"Feminists and bored housewives take note: Sheehan's inaugural volume makes *Desperately Seeking Susan* seem conservative and predictable."—*Kirkus*

"Like Carole Maso, Aurelie Sheehan renders a powerful female sexuality; the prose rushes forward, full of heat and instinct. . . . Aurelie Sheehan should be read, and re-read."—*New York Newsday*

"Sheehan is a real talent."—*Cleveland Plain Dealer*

"Sheehan's gifts are compassion and dispassion, proximity and distance, and her characters are grounded and earthbound."—*Poetry Project*

"Sheehan holds the reader's attention with her insightful look at the crises and tribulations of women, their female sensuality and sensitivity, and their response to male faithlessness. Here is a fine beginning by an enormously important talent."—*Booklist*

"The narrative isn't a road to follow, it's a free-fall, or a floating web that pleasurably entangles the reader. Sheehan's style is lyrical, open and full of metaphorical allusions to the forces of nature and animal life. . . . It evokes an odd mood of beauty slightly out of reach—much the same effect Jane Bowles achieved."—*Cups*

Aurelie Sheehan

JACK KEROUAC
IS PREGNANT

Dalkey Archive Press

Some of these stories first appeared in *Paris Transcontinental, Critical Quarterly, Confrontation,* and *Gutter Poodles.*

Library of Congress Cataloging-in-Publication Data:

Sheehan, Aurelie, 1963-
Jack Kerouac is pregnant : stories / Aurelie Sheehan. —1st pbk ed.
    p.   cm.
    I. Title.
PS3569.H392155J33   1994   813'.54—dc20   94-8742
ISBN 1-56478-262-X

Partially funded by grants from the National Endowment for the Arts, a federal agency and the Illinois Arts Council, a state agency.

Dalkey Archive Press
www.dalkeyarchive.com

NATIONAL
ENDOWMENT
FOR THE ARTS

Contents

With thanks to Gail Somers Sun and Cecily Patterson for insight and solidarity, my parents for their resonant example and my brother Alex for balance, Frederic Tuten for a passionate aesthetic, Tom Horton for his support of my career, the City College of the City University of New York Division of Humanities and Graduate English Department, the Ucross Foundation and Château de Lesvault for providing ways and means, and Steven Moore.

My name *is Aurora Riva. I come from inside. When I am with a man I see more than myself.*

Yesterday I sat in the cab of a truck by the sparkling diamond ocean. The fish were all together in a stream. A silvery indication of something, like a newspaper. I squinted lazily at that beautiful spacious newspaper and read what I could.

And while I read the man next to me talked. I always let my men talk. I give them their voices. And his was a particularly nice sound, low and hesitant and delirious. His was a totem pole flexing, coming together with the earth. Low and gravely, like the ocean shore, the bed of the ocean. He knew I wasn't listening. No, but I let the sounds come to me, one by one, overlapping.

And my eyes left the ocean and drifted over to him. His form hung loosely on the frame. An arm and another arm, on each side of a curving inward and outward, a chest and a tummy. He always had a rounded stomach, this man. And his legs, boyish and polite this time, with white socks and shoelaces tied. But it was his lap I could have crawled into had I wanted a lap at the time.

And his words went on and on. But all I saw was the fabric thrown over the seat of the cab, a tablecloth fabric, triangles and blue wheat. Neither dirty nor clean but a particular homey yeastiness I could have napped in had I been tired.

And then I suppose I said something because he leaned toward me and pushed his sunglasses up and I was facing his eyelashes, a cluster of them, all very dry and attractive. It was then that I first felt myself, my rolling warm belly. I saw also his serious look, an always serious look that takes itself for granted and lives life in a certain way. And the unevenness of his face so that for a minute you wished it were clay so you might change it but then you decide not to, not to even wish it. And he must have said something again here. But all I felt was the dry strong warmth of his hand. A hand I knew rather well over the years, a hand behaving. That hand of his, so different than the hand unclasped. And pirouettes on his thigh and calf by my red-tipped fingers.

How boyish a man can be. And keep that boyishness over the years. As a girl I wanted him to be my man but as a woman I'll let him stay as he is, boy-man, my friend.

And things grew quiet again, I suppose, though the thoughts I said mingled gently with those I didn't say and the water kept coming in.

Jack Kerouac Is Pregnant

I used to believe I knew the future. The future stood in the middle of my living room like a sturdy table. I walked around it. I put things on it—papers, my glass. The table did not move. I vacuumed under it and dusted it. It seemed solid, so I honored it.

I am a pansy. I have always been a pansy. Why? Why is any girl a pansy? It seemed like the road to success. If you're a pansy, someone will come over and help you. By sheer magnetism you will attract a force like rain. My mother was a pansy, too. When my parents divorced, the kitchen faucet broke and that was as mysterious to her as any religious revelation.

The best snapshot of my mother was taken by my father when her skin was tan and smooth and her eyes shone like ivy. She is sitting on a gold velvet chair, wearing a geisha outfit in oranges and yellows, her brown hair pulled back in a wide band. The ends curl up at her shoulders in polite waves. Her smile is placid. She looks like a scarf.

There were lessons I learned in life, as if from a rulebook.

How to Make Love to Your Future Husband

When it is over, sleep dreamlessly. When you wake, drop off your side of the bed without looking in his direction. Go about

1

your business, let the years pass. Watch the dust collect on the bedside table. When he undresses, be aware that his body is of-a-piece: pink, smooth, hot. Yet you do not want it. Least of all is your want for it, most of all is your want.

Be courageous and polite in the face of this. Only get drunk on holidays, don't cry at breakfast.

I stopped speaking when I was five years old. It just seemed like the right thing to do. I wrote short stories on pages of notebook paper and folded them carefully into a drawer.

It wasn't trauma that precipitated this, it was a recognition of the purposelessness of it all. Ask my mother and father and they will say: "Stopped speaking? Untrue—we heard her." That's because I did emit sounds once in a while to keep the machinery in order.

But it was so clear to me that it really didn't matter what I said at all. If I said I wasn't hungry, they said, "Eat your dinner." If I said I wasn't tired, they said, "Nap time, dear."

I wanted to live in a garret and write a novel on one long continuous roll of paper. I wanted a coterie of brilliant, alcoholic friends. I wanted to walk down the street and feel arrogant, and when I wasn't feeling arrogant, I wanted to feel hugely alone, a kind of vast, unending pain that I could challenge with sentences that went on too long.

"I don't want to give you the wrong impression," I wanted to try out on one of the unsuspecting multitude, light a cigarette, and look the other way. What then? Kerouac would hear the wind of possibility in his head like a cyclone and be blown over by the immensity of the present tense.

The feather is brown and black. It is in the hat of the soon-to-be lover, a man I met yesterday, a man who is unlike anyone I've ever met. I am looking at the feather from across the table. He is speaking of something, I don't know what. Words have lost all impact. We are at a bar. In the background, people talk. The TV is not on. It is daytime. We are casually taking sips from our glasses. We are casually reaching for our cigarettes. The clock ticks. And it was only the day before yesterday that I congratulated myself, in sweeping generalizations, on my fidelity to the future husband, the man I have been living with for a lifetime by now, since childhood.

Every Sunday morning we got doughnuts. My father drove to the store and picked them up, huffing and disheveled in the morning. He'd bring back the sweets, rolls and the paper. He ate rolls. I ate doughnuts. My mother—who knows what she ate? She was in the kitchen, doing last night's dishes, swearing. In my nightgown I'd step up to my father as he read the newspaper on the couch.

"Can we do the airplane?"

"Later."

I observed him, his eyes still focused on the printed page. The newspaper was my enemy. I did a pirouette.

"Pretty please?"

"An airplane? Now?" he said gruffly, eyeing me.

"Yes!" I jumped up and down, inclining my head to one side. I knew I had won.

The airplane was our special game.

Dad groaned and put the newspaper down. I giggled. He got down on the floor and put his smelly, knobby feet in the air. I jumped on them. They felt like stones in my stomach, and my feet were in the air now. I was up high, I was flying.

"Whaaaaaah!" I shrieked, when he collapsed his legs and I came toppling down.

"Let's do it again!" I said, and I could hear Mom crashing around in the kitchen, and I knew I'd have to be extra nice to get another airplane ride. I lay on the rug as he picked up his newspaper again. The floor was hard and permanent.

How to Be a Passenger on a Motorcycle

The motorcycle owner gets on the bike. He's stomped on the clutch or whatever that thing is, the choke maybe. He dons his big helmet, puts on his big black gloves, lifts his leg over the hulking machine. He situates himself on the seat, revs, adjusts the mirror, and looks at you, standing on the sidewalk like an orphan. You take the cue. You tentatively put on your helmet, a white one unlike his black one, and you've already put your hair in a braid so it doesn't get too knotty, and you're wearing your white pants and you hope they don't get too dirty. You do a little jump up on the hot leather seat and you are behind him, legs spread, almost prepared. You look down to locate the perches for your feet. You find them as the bike lunges forward, and you are sent back into a fearsome space. You hold onto his jacket and press your face sideways into his back. You know how he feels about the motorcycle. He has told you about the freedom and the adventure.

But you are the passenger. You aren't supposed to lean too much, you are to lean with his body, you are not to make any sudden movements. You therefore tend to look sideways, and the landscape passes by you in a blur. You begin to wonder about your life, about your landlord, about your boss, about the police, about credit cards. You remember a car you once owned and the feeling you had when you drove it seventy miles per hour down a back road. When you remember this, when you remember Pat Benetar on the radio, when you remember the anger, the love, the fear, the pleasure of *that* ride, you smile slightly to yourself, behind the back of the motorcycle driver.

A passenger does not know the curve of the corner the way the one with his hands on the steering wheel does. I think of this on the car ride with the any-minute-now lover. I roll down my window. There is a hawk in the sky. It is early evening. We pass a dead animal on our right. The sky darkens from the tree line up. His hat is on the seat. We have the prospect of swimming before us. I close my eyes for a minute and my head falls back a fraction of an inch, but it feels like a mile. I expect it will rain. He brakes for a stoplight.

This man shocks me. The shock is about words and the body. Speaking becomes a glass of water I hold up to the light. He and I don't know words together. What words we do speak skitter about like lost leaves. It is the pumping tree itself, sap-full and heavy, that we move toward. I have had so many conversations with people across tables in my life. I have chosen words carefully, pulled them out of me like matchsticks and lined them up on the table. With this man whom I move toward with moon-pulled urgency, whom I speak to through my body like an antelope, I am suddenly, shockingly, aware of all the lies I have told. I say, "I want a drink of water," relieved that in this phrase I can find truth. I say, bolder now, "I want you."

How to Be a Future Wife

You must have initiative, first off. Yes? You have that one covered? At parties you stand in the corner and talk to a girlfriend whom you haven't seen for dinner or lunch in months. You talk to her about possibly meeting later. You have a strange urgency in your voice. You have had this urgency before. You had it six months ago when you saw her at another party. Yet you haven't called. You don't even feel particularly ashamed about this, you feel that life goes on forever, you feel that there is ample time to see this friend of yours whom you are squinting at, wondering why you aren't closer.

You envision a life of comfort, ease, security. You have gone to the stationery store and bought thank-you notes and use them on all relevant occasions. "Thank you" the silver script says, and there isn't much space on the inside, so you don't have to write a lot, which is good, because what is there really to say to the future husband's brother, or his mother, or his father, or his grandmother—all these people you have professed love for? "Thank you" is really the motto of your life. Loneliness must be a terrible, terrible thing, you tell yourself, although from your perspective it doesn't seem bad at all.

Politeness is a key aspect of pansyhood. Politeness is like jealousy, it's full of motive but has no result. One of my first lessons in politeness came from my grandfather. We were at a restaurant. The older members of the family, freshly showered after a round of golf, were stirring their drinks with swizzle sticks. I looked at the menu. I was about to order the surf and turf dish, lobster and a cut of steak. My grandfather leaned over and said to me: "I'll tell you a secret. Now, when you are on a date with a boy, the first thing you need to know is to order the cheapest thing on the menu. That way you'll get a husband." I watched his glasses refract while he spoke, I saw his liver-spotted hand move impatiently toward a napkin, I gazed at the firm line of his lips. My mother, sitting next to him, her father, laughed, gleefully as it were. I looked back down at the menu. When it came time to order I asked for chicken. Grandpa remained silent, as if in approval. I was, or would be, a good girl.

Everything is dark. The water is cold. The stones are hard. My legs are thin. There is a rush in this chill, a hurry-up. Underneath the water, out of nowhere, the lover's hands come. His hands are around my waist.

I know things about dreams. I know about words. When he holds me, I am a body. I slow down like a metronome.

I think *the kiss of death* at a pivotal moment. When I go back to the future husband, I feel nauseous with loathing of my circumstances.

A pansy feels odd in the sunlight, however, away from the trees.

*

How to Learn to Dance

You are fourteen, and your femininity has been carefully constructed, a thoughtful composite from magazine articles. There has been a social gathering. You are on the porch, one of the last to leave. You are pretending it is normal to be out after midnight.

He is the bartender. Earlier in the evening he made a comment on your dress. You have cherished the comment for an hour and a half: "You're a cruel woman for wearing that backless dress." He handed you a rum and Coke with a cherry in it. He smiled fiercely, as if he were used to smiling. You put your hand out to receive the forbidden drink and your new cosmopolitan bangle shifted its weight on your wrist, and you smiled back—knowingly, of course. But behind that lightning flash of teeth and your little dance step backward loomed a huge question mark, like a clothes hanger under your flesh, and you had to move around once you were out of his sight, touch your toes and stretch your arms up, to see if you could dislodge it.

It was only this year in psychology class that you learned the term: self-conscious. The word is written in your school notebook on a list with ego, id, animus, infantile and schizophrenic. You hold your stare to the outer reaches of the lawn as he approaches. In this moment you believe something unspeakable has changed in your face and disposition; you are furious with yourself.

"Do you want to dance?" he asks, leaning toward your ear, almost whispering.

You look toward his monstrous smile. You realize it is appalling, but you mistake this for attraction. Yes, you indicate. He takes your hand and you put your other one on his shoulder like you are waiting at a fence. He gently grasps you by the wrist and moves your hand down to his waist. The word *erotic* comes to mind. You will tell your best friend about this.

What were you doing, exactly, to make him say, in his confidence, "Just follow my steps"?

You remember dancing with your grandfather at a fancy restau-

7

rant where old women wore dresses like curtains and their dates wore bow ties around chicken necks. You were wearing a dress with a blue satin bow in the back. You thought it was dumb to have a bow where you couldn't see it yourself. You stood on your grandfather's feet and he danced you around the room, everyone smiled as you went around in circles, it was an enchanted place. On the way out, the maitre d', in a uniform like the bartender's tonight, bowed to you, and you curtsied back.

"Relax," the black and white man in your arms says, and you are trying to do just that. This is enchanting, you think. You have seen another girl over his shoulder, also wearing a backless dress. You smell sweet syrup on the bartender's cuff.

He smiles aggressively when he drops your hand and says he has to go in. You sit down. You feel there is a vague dissymmetry to life.

There are mosquitoes out. You sniff the perfume on your own wrist. You avert your eyes from the scene inside—the dance instructor with the woman in the other cruel dress. Your mother will be here soon to pick you up. In bed tonight you will lie still and flat. You will repeat, "Let him lead," until you fall asleep.

Men and women both like making love for the same reason. But then what happens? She makes a part-time job of wondering if she's pregnant, his mind is breezy like a screened-in porch on Sunday. This is the story:

The man and woman are in the back of the truck, on a wool blanket made by Navajos and reminiscent of sunsets in faraway places. When they touch each other's bellies, heat swims in the air.

Watching the stars move in gentle circles, letting their hands go in the dark night like creamy doves around each other's ears and ankles, they become slowly less aware of what would properly be called sweater weather, and feel the swift upstart breezes only under the hot press of each other's limbs, loins, places of softness and change. The blanket wrinkles like the ocean but neither of them feels the cool metal underneath or the bark and dirt there.

And when her legs are open to the night sky, and he has taken his fingers away from the painting he has stirred and swirled there, they look at each other. He watches her become the earth and then he enters her. She feels his proximity like a glove and then they are together. It is a long smooth moment and to look at the stars or at his face is similar, similar, similar because he is good to her, and their fingers close together like wet leaves and life is there, trembling, unshakable.

It isn't until later when they settle back into their old places that she picks up the newspaper on her chair and reads:

"A drop of life could have leaked from that branch there."

She looks over at the man, comfortable in his easy chair. She looks back, trembling, at the newspaper.

The lover asks me a question and I look away and answer viewing the wall: it is easier. I ask him a question and he sings a beautiful song. The lake is just getting placid. I know there is a feast of trout there, but I can't see underneath the surface. Night falls. I see his hat on the floor.

I wake up later. His hands are on the other side of the bed. We walked over cars in our sleep. We made dents in the aluminum roofs. We laughed. I am looking out the window. A couple argues outside. I hear the argument in sharp focus, and then the voices diminish.

Sex is not polite. Nothing prepared me for it. What kind of sex does a pansy have, after all? Really now. Mellow and subdued, like pressing petals between the pages of a book. A tender fold, a cherished keepsake: dried, faded, flat, perpetual.

Lately I've been seeing young girls on subway platforms holding onto their fathers for dear life. They loll their long brown legs on his panted one, they grab at his stoic arm, they look to his expressionless face for approval. One father leaned over and kissed his girl on the lips. She was so pleased, she let her head drop like a penny down a well.

At the last holiday celebration I spent at my father's, perhaps it was Easter, I watched him tease a three-year-old girl, a friend's child. He pretended to be angry with her. He crossed his arms, knitted his eyebrows together and yelled. I knew he was just joking, and so did the little blonde girl, judging from her composure. She just stood there on her two wobbly, white-stockinged legs, her blue and white print dress ballooning around her, and stared back at this madman, waiting for the withheld item—a piece of a board game, or the answer to a question. His words split the air, the sunny, quietish, afterdinner air, and I was paralyzed. Had I been as confident that the fury was a little joke? Was she even so sure, or was fear running hither-thither behind that imperious stare?

My future husband's, I mean my ex-future husband's psychiatrist said that I was probably from a dysfunctional family, and by breaking up with him I was seeking my own level. "In less than six months," he told him, "she'll hook up with some other dysfunctional person because she is happy with unhappiness and you are just too comfortable and too good for her."

My ex-future husband came home and relayed this explanation of my erratic behavior to me, not saying he believed it, but not saying he didn't believe it either.

How Not to Be a Pansy

Watch a movie about Latino lovers. Imagine yourself in the red dress, shoulder bare, barefooted, flinging furniture. Push the fruit bowl off the table. Throw the wine bottle at the wall. Walk toward and away from the focus of your anger in a choreographed dance. Pack your suitcase quickly, not folding anything, and walk out. Ignore pleas to stay. Break one high heel and keep walking, awkwardly, toward the door.

✳

The ice has melted in the sink, in the room I share with the man who leaves me speechless. There are crannies and crags where the ice was, where the water was, where the air feeds on the mass leaving a lacy sculpture. It is the case of the solid, the fluid, and the air. Absence rings in the small room like an alarm clock. TV in the morning reminds me of doctors' appointments. Around the room are the objects. Lamp. Table. Envelope. Cigarettes. Empty bottle. Bracelets. Money. Car keys. Address book. Airplane ticket.

Airplane ticket? The lover is going on a mysterious and extended vacation.

I have gone into the bathroom and closed the door like a small child. It is the hands holding each other that I will remember, the twist and pressure of our fingers.

How to Be Jack Kerouac

Get rid of all your pillow stuffing—those foam squares you intend, one day, to sew covers for. Then lose your address book. Not intentionally. Leave it on the train in the middle of the night. This must be your only copy. Don't have a previous address book floating around in some drawer—all those addresses are gone, you can't retrieve them, except by chance. (An alternative: drop the address book accidentally into the sea. Pick it out of the water in bold, fine dismay. Turn the wet pages, see how all the letters and numbers are streaked on the paper, blurred together in a watercolor, the new blue scenery of your heart.)

After that, it's OK to go to a bar and sit in a dreary corner and have a beer—so long as you don't give a second thought to what you have just lost, what you once held so dear. You could also lay in bed in your barren apartment and follow the shadows of passing cars. But you must not have feelings at this point. Don't think about the past. Be one with the light, the shadow, the wall.

11

Calculate ways of making intense demands on other people with no intention of reciprocation. Do not concern yourself with what you have just said in passing.

My father forgot my birthday this year. When I told this to my friend she said, "What are you worrying about? My father has forgotten mine for five years." It's one of those Freudian things.

I know one woman who says she just loves her father, they have such a good time together, he is her best friend. I look at her with suspicion and awe. How could such a thing be? Isn't the earth round? I am so used to having a father I can't touch that the other kind appalls me, like a fairy tale come true, like something I have trained myself not to look for and get annoyed to find in the world.

When I am with my father, a thin, sharp edge develops across my back. I sing hello and position myself like a boxer at one side of the room, looking confident. His wife talks to me. He is in the bathroom, or he has lost something of great urgency. I try to be jolly about this, about the missing birthday.

I have bought a car. It is blue. The key to the car is on my desk. I pick up the key and get in the car. I drive out of the parking space. I bank corners. I accelerate. I pass cars right and left. I have an interest in speed and distance, time and space. I contemplate the days of the month. I have numbers in my head, numbers like 28, 29, 30. Numbers like 13, 14, 15. Numbers like 1 in a million. Numbers like 1 out of every 98. Numbers like 2. Numbers like 3. Numbers like 3,800 miles.

The toilet paper comes away white. Days pass.

I had an abortion nine years ago. Last year, walking home to my apartment in New York City, I passed a wall plastered with color photos of dead fetuses, the work of an anti-abortion group. I walked by. I walked back. I studied the photos, the small crunched limbs like bird bones, the eggshell skull cracked in half. I hate any person who photographs, reproduces or plasters up images such as these. I read a book with a first-person account of a woman aborting herself with a knitting needle. I can't remember the verb describing the motion she used. Beat, puncture, grind, knead, pulverize, stroke, thrust—even now I don't know it, the word that goes straight into the cervix and into the womb and into the heart of the fetus. I had to put the book down again and again. I literally couldn't stomach it.

The mailbox is a beautiful void, a clean hollowness. I have asked myself questions about God and about significance. I have looked at the lover's hat hanging on the wall and I have gritted my teeth. I have looked at the hat and I have reached over and touched it. I poke at my breasts several times a day to monitor their tenderness. I roll my fists over my belly like a baby wipes her eyes. My belly feels distended and odd. There seem to be strange shapes inside, a block set, for instance. Sometimes it feels like the shape of a hat.

How to Go on a Date

Ignore the baby mouse your cat brought into the bedroom. Read the advertisement for the perfume you are going to wear. Discuss it with your mother. Wear the dress you found on the side of the road during a light summer shower. Order something with herbs. Smile. Order a drink that reminds you of the lover. Look at your date's lips while he is speaking: wonder. Be silent for the first half of the meal, be loquacious for the second half. Somewhere in between, remember that your childhood heroine was Cher. Remember Cher's stomach. Remember Cher's hair.

Toward the end of the meal, become unaccountably frightened. Start a discussion about the difference between men and women. Talk about your father.

My mother tells me that when she was in college, dating my

father, she climbed a magnolia tree one lethargic day. I can see her skirt falling through the air and her head dropped back, laughing, and her gazelle limbs clutching the twisted branch of the tree. I can see her through the white petals, the flowers that bloom with such radiance only for a few days before withering, like ovulation.

My father looked in her direction, lazy with love, bloated with confidence in the future. It was on this hot day, thighs tacky, underpants moist, that I was conceived—the proverbial accident. There was nothing accidental about it.

The baby's name will be Marcella. She will be a Pisces. The baby and I will move to Montana. I hear it is cold in Montana. The baby and I may move to Texas.

I won't stay home while I am pregnant. I will drive around in my new blue car. I will drive to a different state. I will have a long dusty driveway, a shotgun, a rocking chair. I will be a waitress on the night shift. I will work long and hard hours and know the meaning of life.

My neighbors will keep a respectful distance.

I make an effort to imagine things about Jack Kerouac, to imagine things about road maps. I am defiant on my lawn chair in the backyard. I think: the heart and the body are one. This is the adventure story. You can hitchhike across the country, but if you don't drop the armor over your heart, you haven't gone anywhere. This is the mistake men make more than women, though I certainly have *tried* to make this mistake. You say you are going somewhere. It sounds big and exciting. You can talk about it at the dining room table. You can tell someone all about the roads and vistas. You can even pull out pictures and verify it. But what about a love adventure? What about the peaks and valleys there? No one has pictures of that. The pictures are lost in individual hearts. No one has a map. You can't take the same route.

✳

There is a mountain. There is a cloud. There is a glen. There is a hamlet. There is a cove. There is a tree. There is an indigenous forest. There is a valley. There is a hill. There is a peninsula. There is a natural rock formation. There is a branch on the road. There is my foot. There is my leg. There is my distended stomach.

I quit smoking for the baby. First I smoked six cigarettes in a row in the blue car while stuck in traffic. I crushed the package. The radio wasn't getting good reception.

From the instant I saw the lover I wanted his child. This never happened with the ex-future husband. Never. I could try to forget. I could get an abortion and have a hole in my stomach where the wind whistles through and where, when I walk, I slip into nothing-ness.

The unknown is what I've collapsed into, with my fear. It is not just the question of the sperm meeting the egg for a champagne cocktail on a dark lonely street in the middle of the blue night. It is not just the *if* of that. Pregnancy itself. Conception itself. I do not understand this potential for life landed in my belly. It is my wretchedness in the face of this, the wracking of my brain for an answer to this, that keeps me awake at night.

Abortions cost money; you must wait six to eight weeks into your pregnancy to have an abortion.

I could go to the place I got an abortion previously and have sort of a reunion there.

I have gone to AAA and ordered a travel map for New York to Texas.

Marcella will have blue eyes, like her father.

I find white an absurd, overwhelming color.

15

*

When I was a child, my father came in from a rainstorm one night, wet and full of hate. That day my mother and I had found a sick bird in the yard and put it in the green wicker cage in the front hall. The robin hung listlessly from its perch while my father shook his black umbrella on the portal between home and night. I didn't know if he understood the bird or the bird's plight. Last night, while I was looking through sentimental short story collections from the time when some men thought they knew what life was all about, a little slip of paper fell out. In my father's handwriting, I read this quote:

That which is creative must create itself—In Endymion, I leaped headlong into the sea, and thereby have become better acquainted with the soundings, the quicksands, and the rocks, than if I had stayed upon the green shore, and piped a silly pipe, and took tea and comfortable advice.

This, this is what I want. I forgot. I forgot that part.

The lover who has left me and gone into the unknown, who is traveling in some other country, brought wind into my life and knocked my future over, alchemically changing my life from element to element, from earth to air to fire, and now to water. He helped me remember.

The language between me and this man with whom I plunged into the river, the man who helped ignite the fire that burned the table, the windy man, has made me rethink words.

I know what people will say: You have certainly made a mountain out of a molehill to love this flash of a match, to love this gust. You have certainly taken the high road when it comes to lust.

It is an uncanny new realization for me to be able to say, however sporadically, and to myself, the very thing I want.

I receive a postcard. I am wearing the hat with the feather. I have just come home from buying a small cap for Marcella. I put the cap down when I get the message.

"Wish you were here," writes Marcella, in menstrual blood.

The most fearsome things are unknown to you. They eat away at your reservoir of trout and mustard. They nibble at the edge of the lettuce until it is the size of a radish leaf. This does not mean you should have a fear of the unknown.

Death and birth, naturally, are the great prototypes.

How can you fear something you don't know? This is a question I ask myself as I hike backward, carrying huge fur pelts into the caverns and snowy mountains of myself.

Have you ever cried for something that wasn't pain and it wasn't happiness, either? Just an outpouring of tears, like a migration of birds.

Where does Marcella want me to go? In a moment, I know everything. And in the flick of a wrist, in the death of the caged bird the next morning, in the soar of an airplane out of my life, in the last meal I ate on the hard, firm table of my future before it dissipated into a fine misty ash, in the shock of water, in the change of heart, in the road that turns and is turned from, I will know nothing again.

On the cool, shadowed porch of late afternoon, gray tiles under my feet, trees and lawn stilled in the distance, Marcella talks to me, sings to me: she is an angel. It is in the physical that she grows.

I am and always will be a pansy. My petal is dark purple velvet with a streak of sassy yellow.

17

A Shape in the Water

K asha is smoking and putting on her clothes: the little black underpants that the old lady sells (the old German lady who always calls her dear), string jobs that pull at her hair and lips; the old-fashioned garter belt with new-fashioned fishnets (these never rip—a man could take them in his fists), the skirt that looks like a dress sleeve or a carseat cover when it's off, but she pulls it on, and it hugs her belly and thighs and buttocks. She wears a cross and a Saint Christopher medal. Her wire bra is tight and makes her nipples hurt in the cold weather, but it pushes up and displays her spare flesh.

She stands at the window of her apartment. Her nails, bare of press-ons for the moment, tap on the cold glass. She leans forward and pushes up the window. In the distance a sea gull . . .

A sea gull calls. Desmond looks up from his reading. The imagined blood of men under his nails, he starts, he looks up. He is reading a book about denial and something referred to as destiny. He is reading a book by a woman writing in the eighteenth century. He is reading a book by a woman but, surprisingly, it is fascinating. In fact, it is exciting. In fact, as he sits on a firm leather chair, a chair of brass tacks and cow bellies and curving wooden shanks, his muscles tighten as they did after a day in the field, the

18

dead man's Saint Christopher slicked with blood, and the big feeling Desmond had after cutting him down spreading from his mind to his toes. He reads:

. . . adjoining the sack room, Moll's room . . . against her will, Moll . . . "It was nothing, sir, really . . ."

And he is aroused, only not quite for a woman, but for himself. He lets the book slide off his leg and down to the rug. He follows. On all fours he faces the bear rug. He slumps, he collapses. First he grinds his balls into the bear's snout. Then he unzips and unbuttons and takes it out. As he is performing, he draws the sea gull in, draws it in, tries to remember what it all meant. Because once the sea gull had a meaning. And now? As he rides the quick amusement ride, he forgets, because he is fucking his very best friend, and then the thick cream wakes him up.

It's been a good day. But Desmond is depressed. He'd give anything to remember what it all meant . . .

At the diner, the man behind the counter winks. It is a fatherly wink, but still. The man next to Kasha smells like all men. It's almost enough to make her move down one at the counter. It's almost enough so that she can't stomach the white toast and jelly she's ordered, cooling on a plate with red edges. To get her mind off both of them, she makes an internal list of things she hates more than men. Girls on the street, that's the first item. That's her number one worry. Girls who still don't know where to place their hands as they pace a corner in the city. Girls whose laughter is still disordered, who talk about the future, of aprons and good husbands and good fathers.

Kasha's palm remains folded around the coffee cup as she repeats a litany, *Sex slaves who want to . . . A big mouthful of . . .*

In another place, bent and woven grasses sweater the frosty shore, wrens and sparrows and herons go over the same ground as they did in September, searching for seeds, sporadically, hopefully. The sea gull's wings flap slowly, then hold steady. Light

19

green grasses are shooting up underneath the leaves. Even pebbles stir and turn with the season. Spring is everywhere, but not here in the city.

Kasha leaves the nightclub. She had a notion earlier to talk to men and women as if she were one of them. Reeling, she moves toward a dark corner and leans on a pillar. She faces the building, not the street. She wants—she doesn't want—to be noticed. She was going to take the night off. She is taking the night off. She is a regular woman, an honest woman. She pulled her hair back, applied a paler shade of lipstick, put on a belt two inches across, not six. She wore thin heels, not platforms, the hardy stock. Her skirt is tight but not too tight, she doesn't wear a bra at all. Still, she couldn't see buttoning up her shirt.

She smokes, looking down. When she's cold she feels lost, like she felt when she was a child. Unconsciously, she strikes a pose. In her mouth she tries out the words to a song, a song whispered in the hills, with soil and leaves, and no body to be touched, or sold, or fed. She mouths the words, the size of glass shards. She watches the pavement, her home. Here, the marble smacks of dignity. She concentrates as a tightrope walker would, on the notes.

"Are you alone?"

She looks up. A man as tall as his shadow. Ears sticking out like radar. A soldier's smile.

"I've seen you before," he is saying, looking at her as if looking for someone. Coming closer. She holds her hand up.

"I'm sure you're mistaken."

"No, you look *very* familiar."

His eyes scan her body as he speaks. At the word *familiar,* their gaze meets.

"Maybe I look like your mother?" she asks, bringing the cigarette to her lips.

He catches her wrist. Takes the cigarette. Inhales it once. Flicks it with a vengeance. The ember shoots into the night.

"No, you look like someone I knew in college. A cheerleader. Or maybe my high school sweetheart."

"Good night," she says, jettying herself off the pillar with one foot.

But he has her by the arm.

"C'mon, Kasha. Let me buy you a drink."

Whoring is a multifaceted business, full of middlemen, bosses, and coworkers, but when you're at the car window and the light is turning green, it's just you, you and him.

These days, it's a matter of hotel rooms. She gets a call, goes to the Roosevelt or the Atlantic. Once she went to the Plaza. His wife was on Valium in the next room, could have been dead for all he cared. He wanted to do it on the bar. Took him fucking forever. Kept mumbling about his mother, his wife, a guy called Eddie. *He* was a real winner. From the South. Asked her if she'd ever been to the top of the Empire State Building when he was done, between gulps of vodka. Gave her two complementary passes, but when she was walking toward the door, he grabbed between her legs and hissed, "Your fuckhole is too loose, whore."

Desmond looks into her eyes and Kasha thinks, he is going to kill me. He is the only man in her life.

The words tumbled out of her mouth as they sat, once upon a time, hands interlocked across the table. They were as solid as a fortress in that seedy bar.

"I used to love my pink room. I sat by the window eating peach ice cream and smelling the lilies of the valley outdoors. My dog barked and wagged his tail when I came home from school. The day's mail was placed on the table by the phone in the front hall, I'd check to see if I had any (I considered all cards and catalogs mine), and I'd say hello to the goldfish and drop my books on the stairs."

"We'll have a pink room and a freezer full of ice cream. We'll get a dog. I'll send you lots of catalogs."

21

"Mrs. Olsen next door took about ten minutes to answer her bell. She served me licorice and peppermints from an old silver bowl. We watched thrillers on her black and white television. She wasn't afraid of ghosts. She had a collection of glass animals. She gave me one, a dog strung to three smaller dogs. When I got home I cut the string. Mrs. Olsen died a week later."

"We'll hire someone to take her place, every day you can visit her. She'll live in the guest cottage. I'll do anything for you, Kasha, anything, anything, my love."

"At night I slept with a rabbit skin."

"Is a bearskin good enough?"

His guns were polished, empty and encased. In the next room, Kasha waited. Her feet tickled against the bearskin rug, she lifted one, then the other, to her calves. He had lit a fire. The fireplace was immense, the mantel above her shoulders. It made her feel small, and that was a delicious feeling. She neared happiness, standing on the bear rug, wearing Desmond's grandfather's robe, waiting for Desmond to reappear.

On a table by the bed she saw a Saint Christopher talisman. It was crusted over—with blood? Kasha picked it up and rubbed it against her leg.

Desmond was approaching. Running up the wide mahogany stairs that led to the third floor, his suite, he carried a tray. On it, beside a bottle and two goblets, was a little velvet box. He hurried. He didn't normally. His breath was heavy in the hushed ancestral mansion, everyone either asleep or dead. He was in a panic about the contents of the box.

They made love, the box wide open.

Desmond was crazy in his head with happiness. He padded around the mattress like a wolverine drunk on the scent of fresh blood.

Kasha felt like a slut.

22

In the morning, she put the diamond ring on the bedstand. She picked up the medal and held it in her hand.

Tiptoeing down the steps, she felt small again. But this time the weight of the house was crushing her.

She made it to the driveway. In the dawn mist, the trees were barely visible along the lawn's edge. Her heels sunk and the white pebbles crunched. Somewhere, a gull cried. A window was flung open.

Desmond's mouth was black. His arms flapped like a bird that can't take off.

"Whore!" he yelled.

Other windows opened as she continued to walk. It was a bad movie. The star grimaced.

Kasha bit into the metal so she wouldn't feel the pain. For her taxi fare, she let the old man have his way. She stood, leaning on the yellow cab, and he jimmied around. She squinted out at the white light over the river. She counted. One, two, three, four . . .

It had been years since she and her father stood at Mass, and she asked was there really a God, and he held her neck in his hand, snagging her hair in his ring, jacking her collar up around the throat, and looking ahead, to the altar. Then one day she took a bus, a bus to Broadway. Why, she could be anything: a secretary, a waitress, a slave.

Desmond's race car hugged the curve. He wore sunglasses and music surrounded him as he steered, arms extended straight to the wheel. It was a classical bombast he listened to, full of cymbals and ultimatums. He was wending his way up a mountainous cliff. At the top, he'd smoke a cigarette. But on the other side of this sharp curve, so smoothly negotiated by his automobile, on the sun-steeped black street, a small family of rabbits was slowly hopping across. He saw them as if in a photograph: six rabbits, heads turned toward him, ears pointed up. A big one and her family. In the space of a second, Desmond thought: I didn't realize they traveled *en masse*. How many are there to a litter?

He braked, but not fast enough. Nothing could be fast enough, the rabbits weren't moving an inch.

Cl-cl-clump. He listened as the car went over. He looked in the rearview. Saw nothing. Stopped the car on the side of the road, fifty feet ahead.

As a war hero, Desmond's greatest honor was masterminding a surprise nocturnal attack on an enemy-occupied village. Only one or two civilians were left dead. He was trained to see blood. Still, approaching the spot, Desmond felt agitated. He felt he might burst. What did it matter, his sunglasses, wool pants, Oxford shirt? It didn't help, any of it. He was still as he always had been, just a spoiled little squirt, on a precipice between causing more harm than good.

He began to see the lumps. Scattered on the side of the road, like small dirt heaps. He had thought for a minute that he missed them after all, that the rabbits had gotten their wits about them and fled.

He stopped and looked down. The mother rabbit was dead, her chest flat as a rug. A car whizzed by, ruffling Desmond's shirt. He crossed to the other side of the road. Two babies, dead. And then there was the third, lying on its side, breathing with difficulty. Blood at its nose and mouth. Completely still, the four legs. Just a pathetic breath. It watched him with a glassy, nervous eye. In a frantic spasm, the half-dead rabbit attempted an escape. It got up, fell, got up again—and collapsed. Desmond reached down and touched it. When he laid his hand on the wild fur, the animal seized up for good. In the grass, ten feet away, Desmond heard a scrambling. It was the last two, hopping away.

With unsoldierly abandon, Desmond got in his car and turned back home.

✳

Kasha's given up. Her chest feels smashed, as if blood is rising to the surface.

Desmond follows her, his head bent against the wind. When she left him, he felt he'd lost what made him a great soldier. No society gal could do it, no coiffured blonde horsewoman or quick-witted Vassar grad. No joy in the kill, the conquest, the action. He fell into a lassitude. He was unwell. Following Kasha down the dark street, he recalls now what he once was, what he thought of himself as.

"I'm not what you think I am. I'm not what you want," she yells over her shoulder.

"I never loved anyone but you."

"I can't love you."

"You're lying to me."

Kasha turns around and faces him.

"Listen, I only do it for the money."

"But you don't have to."

"And you don't have to be a soldier."

"I'm not even a soldier, anymore," Desmond says, looking down. "What are you going to do with the rest of your life, Kasha? What are you going to do when you get old?"

"Don't you see? Even if I have no customers, I'm sold."

"It's not true! I know for a fact it's not true! It doesn't have to be! We could be together!"

But Kasha is walking away from him.

Desmond's whole family wept thrilled tears of pride and morbid foreboding when he chose active service in the war. "No desk job for him," his mother proudly asserted, between mouthfuls of crudités, loudly and impatiently at charity dinners, balls, intimate teas with two or three others, the same mother who had begged him to take his father's route: using the simplest, most discreet means to assure his continued health and, indeed, life; taking the opportunity afforded him by their position: to maneuver a niche in a safe haven where he could play billiards, keep his shoes shined, and build up the muscle on his small frame.

When he first shot someone Desmond had a feeling, a thrill at the play of a new fetish, the ugly and ecstatic thrusting in. He looked around almost guiltily. This was how it was done?

"Go man," the Major growled in the trenches, punching him forward.

And it was all right. So he shot again and again and again.

It is April but the sweet air enters Kasha's nose like poison. Trash swirls in a whirlwind in front of an out-of-business stationery store. Cardboard leprechauns, valentines, Christmas reindeer shuffle together like playing cards. She steps over them. Searching for the key to her building, Kasha hesitates at the door. One, two, three, four . . .

Through the scope, you can see a beaver swimming in the lake. The surface of the water is smooth, reflecting the sky, except for a spot, slowly moving forward. A V-shape widens behind the animal. You can see the V-shape and that is how you know she is there. But the animal thinks she is secure. She swims quietly. Only everyone can see the arrow, the whole lake is pointing at her.

The Bone Man

M y mother called me Scarlett because when she was young
and unbeaten down, when her skirts and blouses resembled
her underthings of later years, she used to read the American
movie magazines. She thought Atlanta was the capital of the
United States, and Scarlett O'Hara breathed that cotton air. My
father didn't really care what they called me; Mama had gotten as
close to a Rhett Butler as possible in a small South American
country with a class structure sinister as a whalebone girdle. She
had never seen the insides of the shapely, chintz-lined mansions,
they were as silky and far-off as the look in her eyes when she
circled white powder between her breasts and imagined the hero-
ism of men in movies. Papa was tall and dark, to begin with, and
he had a clever smile. He always had something in his pockets,
either a bag of gumdrops for me, or a handkerchief for Mama, after she found him in their meticulously arranged bed with some
little girl he pulled in from the market. All his women were
grown-ups to me, but when I look back on it, I know that those
mussed-hair *chiquitas* who stopped in their tracks when they saw
me in the garden and frowned as if they had just remembered
some vital link missing from their nighttime reasoning, were only
a few years older than I was, in my bare feet and banana-colored
nightgown.

I smiled at them as they hurried away from my house, and then I looked back down to pull off a beetle from underneath the thick, shiny leaves of the pepper plant or the corn. The yellow and black striped beetles always nuzzled closer into the stem of the leaf when they saw the shadow of my hand. My mother told me to crush them, but I let them go by the side of the road, with instructions never to return. Mama and I both planted and tended the vegetables and the flowers, but most summertime evenings she would send me out alone with a basket to pick three of one thing and two of another in the dull quiet of dusk before Papa came home. She waited until seven for my father to arrive (he closed his store in town at five), and if he didn't show up, she threw his portion of dinner into the garbage can, while I tried to swallow what she had slapped down before me, muttering obscenities, prayers, and proclamations about life on the plantation, and real gentlemen.

I don't remember seeing my mother eat at all. Even when Papa did come home on time, which happened on occasion, she merely sat next to him, waiting to serve his next course, watching him with a glower that went wet often. He was so handsome, and nonplussed by her bowed head or remonstrances. He might begin a story, "Adolfo arrived late again this morning. I would have fired him but he had a guilty look on his face that promised some fun. Before I could ask him about it, his wife came in, yelling something about the spiritual education of their children. She was waving a porcelain Mary around her head like a club. It was only then that I saw he had a blackened eye, bruised by the effigy of a Virgin." He held out a hand and caressed my mother's chin, cajoling a smile out of her early-years pout, the frown that later became chiseled into her skin.

My father sold rugs, brass and lamps. His was a nonessential store in a town of one thousand citizens. Business went well in waves. Rinaldo, who was fat and freckled and saw prostitutes, might come in just to talk to my father, worried that his wife was having an affair when she should be bleaching the tiles of the front hall, or smoothing down the cloth on his kitchen table. My father would convince the imagined cuckold that a pair of candle holders would be just the thing to keep her legs shut and her hands attending to sponges and his own speckled stomach. And so the sale was made. But sometimes the men just came in for titillation. My father could tell a story of seduction that left his lethargic neighbors gasping for air. And he always ended with one line about my mother, or so Adolfo told her much later: "But not even she comes close to María, who has the touch of fire and a tongue of water."

What kept my father in business was liquor, which he sold under the table. He imported it from the United States, and he had even been there once. On their first date, he undressed my mother with tales of this trip, and on their wedding night she was still thinking of Houston, Texas, and New York, New York.

One day my mother went from turning the pages of the American magazines to turning over tarot cards. She came home from shopping that afternoon and set a card deck on the kitchen table, by the oranges and the flour. I was at the table, watching her. I had been arranging the oranges into a circle around the flour sack, with a tail of lemons and a lime at the end. I grabbed the big box of cards. It was the size of a novel in my small hands.

"What's this?" I asked.

"Nothing," she answered, starting to bang things around for dinner. She often acted as if she were in a rush, as if the physical properties of the world had somehow slighted her.

The picture on the package depicted a young man at a table. In front of him were a series of objects: lemons, limes, flour is what I saw. In the background stood a red tree, ripe with violets.

"May I open it?" I asked.

"Go ahead," she said in a crisp voice and went back to chopping vegetables.

I tore the plastic wrap off the box and opened the cardboard flap. A little piece of paper fluttered out and fell to the floor.

"What's that?" she asked. So she had been watching me after all.

"These cards . . ." I began to read in small print on the folded piece of paper before she took it out of my hands and read it to herself.

"Hmm," she said, putting it in her apron pocket.

(Later I checked that pocket: "These cards are for playing purposes only. No one may profit from the practice of the tarot. The future is unknown to all but the divine.")

I had just spread out the cards when she said I was to put them away and clear the table for dinner. She put the cards in a drawer.

Dinner took forever that night. My father had brought home a bottle of wine, which he opened with a flourish, holding it in one hand as he swung Mama around for an alcoholic kiss, his breath hot on her cool skin.

"Did Carlos buy the carpet?" she asked, setting the soup down after Papa had joined me at the table.

"No."

Silence, accompanied by the sound of cutlery clinking.

"And what about the payment to the bank?" she said five minutes later.

"We'll manage it."

That was the first course.

"The boys are planning a party for Friday night down at Juan's. It's going to be an American party, with fireworks and beer and hamburgers. Have you ever seen fireworks, Scarlettina?"

"No! What are they?"

"They are like little suns that rise and set in an instant. They make a big noise, like Papa falling off his bicycle after a long night of drinking."

I giggled, hiccuping into my milk. He looked over at my cold, silent mother.

✳

I followed Mama upstairs into her and my father's bedroom after we finished cleaning the kitchen, and Papa was reading the paper in the living room. I knew she had the cards. She began undressing while I sat on the bed. She slipped off her black stockings and left them crumpled near my hand. I pulled them toward me and extended my thin, bare arms into the still-warm folds.

"You monkey," she laughed, grabbing at one of the wagging legs.

She took off her dress, her camisole, her underpants, and put on her nightgown and robe. Then she sat down on the bed next to me and took out the deck.

"I have to earn some money myself or you will never make it to the United States," she said.

"But I don't want to go there."

"Don't be silly," she said, shuffling the cards. And then she added, "Go on to bed."

In my room, I listened to the chatter of the television from downstairs where my father sat in the flickering light, and I imagined I heard my mother shuffling and laying down the cards, talking quietly to herself about the future. I closed my eyes and saw the primary colors of the stern little pictures in which you could see yourself.

The next morning I woke to my parents arguing.

"How can you have so little faith in me, your own husband?"

"I have nothing but faith in you."

"Do you believe this supernatural shit?"

"I saw my own life very clearly in the cards last night."

"What does that include, a new lover?"

"No. They tell me I have a beautiful husband, with blond hair and great ambition."

My father grabbed a lock of his hair and held it in a tight, shaking fist.

"This hair is black, black, black!"

"I know, darling. I need practice."

My mother smiled and walked up to him. She put her hands on his chest.

"I need to do this. I spoke to Saint Clare about it."

He looked down at her, and his lips and jaw quivered, then set in place.

That's when I saw the painted sign drying on the porch. "Spiritual Readings," it said, in a thin blue script.

The customers came slowly in the beginning. Señora Ramón and her backward son were the first to stop off, but they didn't pay to get their cards read.

"Well, María, so you've decided to do something besides dream about the United States?"

"I never dreamed about it any more than I do now."

"But you've found something to occupy yourself?"

"Saint Clare came to me while I was chopping carrots and told me to buy a pack of cards."

(This became my mother's standard response. Whether it was true or not I really didn't know. She had always prayed to Saint Clare, but sometimes, while praying, she looked at her watch.)

"And you're charging money, just like a real fortune-teller?"

"Yes."

"How much?" Señora Ramón asked, turning to her son, who had just let out a sort of bellow. She began wiping his face ruthlessly with a cloth she produced from the pocket of her housedress.

My mother mentioned a price, at which Señora Ramón balked and snorted herself.

"Do you need anything from town, María?" she asked, then continued her stiff parade down the road, holding her gawky, lovely son by one hand. He looked to all sides as she narrowed her eyes to the horizon.

32

I sat by my mother on the porch most of that first morning, learning how to shuffle and lay down the cards. She didn't get any business, and at lunchtime she sighed and went in. I wandered over to the garden and began marking the border with small stones. Señor Perez, the old bachelor who lived just down the road, came by on his bicycle when I was about a third of the way around the garden's perimeter. He slowed down, and I could see he was trying to make out the words of her sign, he was mouthing the sounds. Then he got back on the seat of his bicycle and rode on.

The next day, when the white, smooth stones encircled almost the whole garden, Señor Perez returned. This time he rode his bicycle up to the porch and leaned it against the house. He hadn't seen me where I was squatting by the side of the porch, digging for more stones.

"Is anyone home?" he yelled. He was a little hard of hearing.

My mother appeared in the doorway.

"Are you open for business or not?" the old man roared.

My mother said yes, and he maneuvered his way up the stairs.

In a few moments I heard the scratch of a wooden match against flint, and then I heard a soft murmur from my mother; it was the nervous, slightly disappointed whisper of her prayers.

"Saint Clare, Saint Clare, Saint Clare," she said, but the words were indistinct and sounded like a whoosh and cluck, not a name at all.

"Cut the cards into three piles . . . no, with your left hand," she said, and Señor Perez grunted in response.

I heard the cards slapping down on the table. By this time I had sat down against the frame of the house, my breath held in, waiting. . . .

"There is a woman who opens the window in the early morning and puts her head out to smell the dew and to hear the birds' song. She has cultivated a life without danger. That woman is you,

Señor Perez. But there is a feeling of want here . . . a lack, a lack. . . . There can and must be victory for you, so long as you open your heart to the world as if it is a lover."

There was a moment or two of silence. I could hear Señor Perez's labored breathing, each breath coming slowly, far removed from the others.

"There is always more for you if you can allow your knees to bend, to ride with the shape of the horse. You are an old man, perhaps, but you are strong. Act wisely, be patient, regard setbacks as stepping stones."

I heard the slide of the cards coming together and a sharp slap when she put them down.

As Señor Perez passed me on the stairs, I saw a wild anguish in his eyes and a deep, unleashed sorrow in his gaping.

After he died, they found a pile of love letters in his house, all addressed to María.

My mother became a bit of a sensation. Even Señora Ramón got off her high horse and came to get her fortune told, while her son swung his head this way and that on the white porch steps. But one of my mother's most frequent customers was Señorita Ventura, who always came back.

Señorita Ventura was my schoolteacher. She had a sad look under her glasses and her thin brown bangs. She walked as if she were coming from a great distance. She visited my mother often, sometimes once a week, until her sudden death. I heard through the kitchen door what happened. She went to a bar in town one night, alone. It was unusual enough for a woman to go to a bar like that, but Señorita Ventura hadn't been out after sundown since she had moved to our town two years before. That night she ordered a full bottle of the strongest liquor in the house. She oriented it on the bar in front of her, pulled out a pack of cigarettes from her little purse, poured a shot, lit a cigarette and drank. The men at the other end of the bar exchanged glances as she systematically and demurely belted down drink after drink. At the end of two hours, she left. She walked more boldly on her way out. The next day they found her body in the river, her packed suitcase by the grassy bank, at the bus stop.

My mother had read her fortune just the day before, so naturally everyone wanted to know what had been said. My mother was silent. She shook her head slowly and surely, her eyes on the table.

When everyone had left, I asked her myself.

"I told her she was going to be a virgin all her life," she said and shrugged. "I guess the cards were right."

I woke up one morning and my mother wasn't in the kitchen. She was sitting on the steps of the porch, stroking the branch of a dark-leaved tree with her long fingers. I went back upstairs to my parents' bedroom. I walked up to the bed and looked at the sheets twisted together and the two pillows, crushed and crunched into one heap. I put my hand on the pillowcase, the fabric wrinkled finely as a baby's palm, smooth as skin to the touch. I looked back, then, at the door. My father's cane, the one carved for his father, always hung from that doorknob. Papa didn't use it, except for on Sundays, or New Year's, or other special occasions. The cane wasn't there.

I guessed that the brilliant white above the treetops in the distance told my mother a story she hadn't seen in the major arcana, or the profusion of cup cards she had been receiving lately. I guessed that was it for Papa.

That was the day Saint Clare and the Bone Man married each other. My mother, taking the bull by the horns, was throwing out the possessions that didn't make it into Papa's suitcase (also missing, we found later). I saw shadows of lobbed clothing fluttering down from the upstairs window. Papa's shirts filled with air, then lay in a colorful heap on the ground.

I walked over to the round table on the porch where my mother told fortunes. I pushed over and spread out the well-thumbed pile of cards. From between the Knight of Swords and the Emperor, one card called to me. It was the Bone Man. He was card number thirteen, with a wisp of a flower in the foreground, just the touch of life. He was a lonely figure, creeping through a field of skulls with that cane, that sickle, in his hand. Customers were always turning pale as the inside of a coconut if my mother flipped him up from his nap. "Something will end," she said to the ones she liked. "You cannot prevent it." I tilted my head to one side and looked into his cavernous eyes. I could be his friend.

I brought the card with me to the garden. I walked in the gate, past the four rows of corn. At the end of the garden, surrounded by looming, bent-headed sunflowers, Saint Clare's statue and a bird-bath nestled in the cool morning shade. I sat down by her and wrapped my arms around my bare knees. Saint Clare's face, etched roughly in granite, looked beneficent, but far away. She had her arms spread, but they were empty. Maybe the Bone Man could change that. He, too, needed someone to embrace in the night. The other cards had turned their backs on him, and he had to shuffle off into the corner in his grim underpants.

"You two were meant to be together," I whispered, placing the card by the granite saint.

"Saint Clare, Saint Clare, Saint Clare," I repeated on the plane, my hands folded in front of me, as if in prayer.

I had never seen the land from that perspective before. I held my straw hat in my lap, the hat I needed with me despite the pro-testations of my mother and my best friend from high school, Celia.

"You won't need a hat like that in New York, my dear," Celia had said in my bedroom the night before. She was cosmopolitan in a certain sense—she wore Revlon eye shadow and knew the weight of Elizabeth Taylor—but she herself was going to stay in

36

town, and move in with her fiancé above his father's shop as soon
as she finished school. My mother laughed with Celia, giddy
though she couldn't know what I would need in New York. Still,
Mama felt she had a right to my future. After all, it was she who
had grabbed my hand one day and peered closely at its contents.
"College, in the United States," she had said. And I believed her.

I stared down at the hat, afraid to look out at the earth swinging
back and forth as if seen from upside down on a gymnastic bar. I
was thinking about Manuel's hands. They had felt their way under
the green and blue fabric of my uniform, they had taken the braid
my mother wove on Monday morning and unraveled the three
strands slowly and with breathless deliberation. We had spoken
together, on the bandstand, about the curve of the playing field,
about the ridge at the end where you could see the stalks of grass
growing, and then there was nothing. He thought life was like
that, green and shiny until the end. Now the earth rocked underneath me and I wondered. What I still wished for, and wished for
with such intensity and such a feeling of impending death, was to
plant a seedling in the moist earth, to tumble the dirt mound into
the hole, to pat the surrounding soil with my hand, and to knock
the black dirt from the two green leaves, reaching upward.

For my first few months in New York, I was to stay with my
Uncle Mercado. He was my father's brother. He owned a restaurant and a pizzeria, and he was involved in other business that my
mother and I couldn't fathom from the other side of the continent.
After my father left us, Mercado sent Mama yellow roses on her
birthday and chocolate at Christmas. The only time I had met him
was when he came to visit when I was ten. He arrived without
warning, driving up in a limousine that he rented all the way from
the airport. Some of the neighbors looked out their doors and windows at him. They were already formulating rumors about my
mother when the back door of the car opened and they recognized
Mercado, who had grown up there, like my father.

Mercado sat in my father's chair at dinner. I sat with my hands under my legs, except for when I took a perfunctory slurp of stew at extended intervals. The Bone Man was on the table. I had propped him up by the blue glass, the one my father used to drink from. I was talking to the Bone Man silently about things while Mercado charmed my mother. That evening, after eating my mother's flan, Mercado wound out a story meant for my pleasure. He told of a little girl who slept in a garden and a big dog that wanted to eat her. When she saw the dog, she wasn't frightened, but just shrugged her shoulders and went to sleep. The dog was baffled. He didn't know what to do, so he curled up and slept beside her, determined to guard her from bad dreams all night long. "Tell another!" I said when he was through, and I put my creased, reddened hands on the table.

"No, Scarlettina, go to bed now," Uncle Mercado said.

I gave the sweet-smelling man who had called me the name only my father used a kiss on his wide cheek, above the silk collar.

But that was years before, and now I was meeting Uncle Mercado at the airport. Out beyond the customs gate, a swarm of people leaned in toward me. I walked forward nervously, not knowing where to look, amazed at all the small white signs scrawled with names or numbers.

"Scarlettina!" rang through the air.

Out of the crowd, a man came forward. He was large, well-dressed, and carried a cane. In that first instant, as the gray-haired man moved toward me, I thought he was Papa, whom I had secretly done all my homework for. He had come to the airport to see me. We would live together. He had been following my progress from afar, he knew about my decision to go to school, he was there—

But then, as I was running toward the open arms of this man, I saw that it was, in fact, Uncle Mercado.

"Hello, Scarlettina," he repeated, his voice clearly now not my father's.

Mercado pulled me toward him. My face was turned against his smooth, tan jacket as he embraced me with gusto. "Pa—," the first syllable, hung in the air.

In one day I went from a final barefoot walk through the garden at home to sitting across the table from a man whose fingernails were the color of the tablecloth and shined like the glassware in a fancy uptown restaurant. Uncle Mercado spoke to me about what he thought I wanted to hear: Graceland, Disneyworld, Niagara Falls. Perhaps he thought I was my mother? His smile popped up unexpectedly between words or sentences, after a gulp of his brownish cocktail, or a crunch of ice between his straight white teeth. His face was tired, as if he needed a big dog to guard his dreams now. I leaned forward, eager for a whiff of Mercado's pressed and starched shirt, of the reptile-skin watchband, of the cologne that was so different from outdoors.

New York held its own surprises, was its own person. While Mercado hailed a cab after dinner, I stood in front of his restaurant on a street full of cars and people, and I looked up at the coffin-shaped patch of sky above all the buildings. I took a breath. This city was a giant—brilliant, illuminated, dangerous. He leaned over me, his arms like pillars on both sides of my head.

In those first August days, it was hot and steaming on the streets, and the air smelled of urine, and even a gust of wind had soot in it, which got in my eyes, and I had to look down at the sidewalk again. This new lover of a city ran his brutal hands down my arms and legs, possessing me thoroughly. I looked wildly into people's faces and thought of my mother, of what she loved and dreamed into this part of the world. I could see a dream in the faces of these people who walk everywhere, and I could see it slip out of sight, on the straight, straight roads that curve imperceptibly under your footsteps.

꙰

My uncle had a crucifix over the fake fireplace in his living room. It was large and ornate, and the red paint slathered on for the bloody patches was chipping off the plastic. Our apartment was in the basement, so if you looked out the grated windows onto the street, you could only see people's lower halves. From this perspective it looked as if the disembodied calves and feet could take off if they chose to, like angels. On a bureau by the window, there was a car part of some kind, a jar of industrial poison, a set of chopsticks, and a vase of paper flowers with red stamens the size of matchsticks. I waited in this room for my uncle to come home the day of registration at school. I had lost my raincoat. I had left it in one of the innumerable bathrooms in the biggest of the big buildings on campus. In the spare, masculine bathroom here at my uncle's, my cotton balls, facial cleanser and hairbrush looked peculiar.

Mercado's keys finally danced on the other side of the black door, and his beery face leaped into my consciousness. He smiled ingratiatingly, took off his wrinkled-at-the-armpits linen jacket, shook it a bit, and hung it on the back of one of the dining room chairs.

We had dinner. He made hamburgers, saying I deserved to be cooked for after dealing with the university's bureaucratic shuffles. He drank beer in the kitchen, surrounded by smoke from the burned beef under the broiler. After we ate, he rotated his glass, smeared with fat from the meal, in one hand.

"Scarlett," he said, "You look like a crystal-clear lake in the sunshine, lapping slowly on the shore. Having you here, I can almost smell our country in the air. Yes, but how much more useful water is when it is bottled for drinking, or channeled into a mill to harness its energy into real power. That is what the U.S.A. is all about—making use of what you are."

"Have you heard from my father?"

I held my breath.

"I talked to him last winter. He was in Texas . . . an oil well or some crazy thing. He loves you," my uncle added, twisting his lips.

"I'll do the dishes," I said, getting up.

"You and your mother," he continued, as I cleared the table.

I began working at Uncle Mercado's pizzeria. He was rarely there, but I could feel him in the big vats of grated cheese that looked wormy if you felt under the weather, or the floods of tomato sauce, thick as quicksand. I was the only woman working there, and the cook and his helper sidled up to me behind the counter as I counted pennies for customers. I wanted a new job.

There were thousands of fortune-tellers in this city, big signs advertised the future for five, ten and fifteen dollars. One day I was waiting to cross the street, and I saw in the second-floor window of a building on the other side a sign that said "Spiritual Advisor Needed." I could see people moving around in the window like hairdressers. I missed the walk signal and decided to apply.

"Would you like your fortune told today? Do you have an appointment?"

"No, I came about the job."

"The job? Do you have experience?"

"Yes," I said vaguely. I felt experienced and inexperienced both.

"Have a seat. Madame Lisa will be right with you."

A plain-faced woman with bleached-blonde hair tacked up on her head in random fashion looked over from one of the tables when the receptionist said this. She had someone's hand in hers. I sat down and began reading a fashion magazine.

Madame Lisa was of European origin. She wore a red satin robe and stretchy pants. She was my mother's age, and her fingernails were polished in two different colors. She called me over to

41

her booth. (There were about eight women working in this room. Each had a table, one chair for the customer and one for herself, as well as an array of lurid objects—red candles, fur pieces, icons.) Madame Lisa passed me a pack of tarot cards and said:

"Let's see what you can do."

I took the cards in my hand and whispered Saint Clare's name over them. I asked Madame Lisa to touch the cards. She did so with a sharp flick of her wrist. I laid out the ten cards and gave her a reading, staying as close to the standard definition for each card as I could remember. Laying them out was a pleasure, it was like looking at snapshots from my childhood.

When I was done she snatched up the cards and looked at me with her smeared brown eyes.

"We don't go for hocus-pocus here, you should know that. You'll get a good commission on each client, but you've got to do them quickly, and you've got to know what to say. You can't make things out like they are fixed, you have to give the client a hook. Get them thinking about something—sex is always good. Or money—an inheritance, whatever. Giving one reading isn't nearly as important as making the appointment for the next. That's *our* future. Got it, cookie?"

"Hey, Madame!" the receptionist yelled from across the room. "You've got to talk to this lady. She wants to cancel for tomorrow."

"Shit," Madame Lisa said. "I'll be right back."

While she was gone, I watched the woman next to me tell a fortune to a collegiate-looking girl. The fortune-teller lit a candle, swung the cards around the air as if she were practicing a golf stroke, raised her eyes to the ceiling and invoked Jesus. I listened coldly to her recitation: a career change, a new lover, money from afar. All the time I was thinking about my mother. This city didn't always watch what it was doing, things got out of hand underneath its mountainous body if a woman could pretend to be something she wasn't, and money would defend the sloe-eyed impersonation.

"I'll give you a chance, ten o'clock tomorrow morning," Madame Lisa said, standing next to me with her hand outstretched.

"I'll think about it," I said, getting up.

We shook hands—hers was dry as a mannequin's.

"You won't find a better deal in town. Where are you from, anyway? You just came to the city from someplace?"

I told her where I was from.

"Oh, a lovely place, lovely. But things here are different, more businesslike. You see? We work quickly and efficiently. You give the client what she wants, got it? You'll do well," she added in a low tone, her hand on my arm. "You think about it, and call me."

I walked back down the dusty staircase, under the palm reading/tea leaves/crystal ball/tarot cards marquee. It was back to the pizzeria.

One late afternoon in October, I decided to visit Uncle Mercado at the uptown restaurant. I had received an A on my first history paper and I didn't want to go back to the quiet apartment and watch TV. In front of the restaurant, a gust of wind blew my hair and new raincoat into a swirl. I opened the glass door, stepped into the foyer and smoothed my hair. When I opened the second door into the restaurant, I was instantly warm, and the dimly lit, glimmering room had a holiday feeling. I was beginning to unwrap the scarf from around my neck when I looked toward the bar. A man was sitting there, having a joke with the bartender. The bartender was holding a jar of olives in his hand. The man with his back to me chuckled. Perhaps the bartender had made a joke about jars, about women, about olives. In that chuckle there was a claw.

"Papa?"

The man swung around. A look of terror became a smile.

"Scarlett," he said, standing up, coming toward me.

There was a flash of pure life, like a hawk alighting from a bare tree at dawn, and then there was silence.

"I just got into town, I was going to surprise you tonight," he explained with a death grin, holding my arms in his hands.

I smiled back. When a person has smiled at you, yes, you smile back.

He held me. I thought my stomach was heaving from happiness, but I was nauseous. I broke away from the embrace and ran to the bathroom.

I vomited instantly. When it was over, I turned my gaze from the putrid white toilet to the mirror. The Bone Man would love me, I said to myself, falling back against the wall, lifting my chin, looking at my reflection through half-closed lids. The Bone Man is the one for me, not this fleshy father.

I sat at the bar with Papa, a bowl of peanuts between us, a glass of wine in front of me and a scotch in front of him. I could only look at him in snatches. His cheeks, now like a grandfather's. His lips, pursed as if he were remembering something he had left at home, an umbrella or a pair of gloves. His thinning hair. His eyes. They hadn't aged at all, his eyeballs I mean. I looked into the dark pools, the eyes I had savored in my dreams for a decade, and saw nothing.

He asked me about school, about New York, about my friends at home. He asked me all the right things. I gazed at the tops of the bottles behind the bar where they stood like skinny mountains.

At some point, much later it seemed, or maybe it was only an hour, he said he had to go. I nodded as he told me about a business meeting and about calling tomorrow to arrange dinner before he went back to Texas. When my father put on his gray coat, I said: "Mama is doing fine."

"Oh, is she?" he said. "Good."

He was buttoning his coat and smiling at my uncle at the same time.

When he left, Mercado asked me to stay at the restaurant for dinner. I said no.

✱

The streets were dark by then, and the wind had died down. The chill of the evening felt good to me. I left my raincoat unbuttoned. Looking around at the people on the street, I knew everything about them, down to the last thread of their last shirt button, down to the whisper in their ear. I thought of Atlanta, burning, and how my namesake kept walking.

You've seen women sitting alone at the end of dark bars, slow, poisoned embers in their guts, drinking? Well, every one of them has a story, or so I told myself, sitting, drinking, forgetting the future and the past. It was just the present for me, here in a half-filled glass, a just-lit cigarette, in my freshened lipstick, brushed hair, the jagged run in my stocking. I switched my leg position from left over right to the reverse, smoothed the napkin, stared off at a distinctly dark spot on the paneled wall across the bar. I was imagining my mother's shoulders shifting with gentle precision under a thin white blouse, her back to the kitchen table, doing the dishes for me and my father.

"Don't you want to see the match?" said a voice near my ear.

I turned toward the man who had spoken. There was something unbalanced in his face.

"What do you mean?" I asked.

"On TV, honey, what do you think? Where are you from? Where's your date?"

These questions came one after the other, and I was confused by them, confused by conversation. I looked at this man's face, searching it for information. His eyes, relatively small in a cluster of wet, black eyelashes, were unknowable. His skin was tanned and leathery, but there was something delicate about the hollows of his cheeks. The ridge above his top lip curved like a ballet step. His nose was a bit of a problem—it must have been broken once or twice or three times. It was shaped like a question mark.

I looked up at the boxing match on television. The man grinned and took a sip from his clear red drink. He sat down next to me, his eyes on the TV over my head. I looked into my drink, and thought about ordering another, and thought about lighting a cigarette, and thought about breathing. In about a minute he knocked me on the knee with the back of his hand.

"Well?" he said.

"Well what?"

"Where are you from? You have a delicious accent."

That ember inside ignited with his breath, with the fanning of his clumsy, casual hands which found themselves passing over my body in small accidents. Soon I knew the smell of his skin. I felt the proximity of his arm around the back of my bar stool, I saw his dirty nails and the calluses on his hand when he paid for my next two drinks from a wad of crumpled bills he got out of his front pants pocket. His shirt was wrinkled too—a crinkly, cotton Oxford. I took off my coat and sweater. The cool air from the fan brought goosebumps to my flesh.

He didn't have his own apartment, or someone was staying at his place, or he was from Boston; anyway, something required that we tiptoe through a dark apartment, stumbling over chairs and tables. Finally we reached a little room and he closed the door behind us and wrapped his arms around me in a hundred different ways, like an octopus. We fell over, undressing. We bent this way and that, and I felt his wet, greedy tongue, his soft hair, his hot skin, and that thing, insistent and alive between his legs. The room was dark except for a brilliant white illumination.

In the morning, this man's eyes, which had at first seemed impenetrable, and then were only mysterious, were back to impenetrable again. This time the absence was frightening. He had woken me by shaking my arm and whispering hoarsely that we had to leave right away before so-and-so who owned the apartment woke up.

I dressed quickly, aware of a headache like a flashy collar around the back of my head. I put on my coat and I picked up my backpack, the one with the paper no one had seen in it. He hurried down the stairs in front of me, a jaunty, knee-bent gait, cigarette smoke wafting periodically from one side of his body. I descended more slowly.

"Saint Clare," I whispered, watching his form move away from me down the road, lost in puzzle pieces by another person, a trash can, a lamppost. It was early. The sifted gray of ashes, a light like new birth, pulsed at some distance. "This is the cool, deadly look in your marble eyes. This is his bony embrace."

Each bite of my uncle's pancakes tasted like sawdust and felt like lead going down. Mercado had been asleep when I pulled the heavy keys out of my purse earlier that morning and crept past his bedroom into my own. Now he poured me orange juice like it was going out of style.

"My father should be calling today."

A look of fear passed across Mercado's face, and I knew why he had made pancakes that morning.

"He's a busy man, your father. Busy and wonderful," he added, looking off into space.

I didn't really care. I only felt the throbbing between my legs, the regal fog surrounding everything. That man was a hard, precious thing, and my hand was still open from letting him drop into the murky pool.

I spent much of the day watching a Laurel and Hardy movie on television, waiting, though I knew not to wait; waiting, though the thought of my father not calling was too much to bear, and though I knew this was what would happen; waiting, though the task of waiting, the possibility of his calling or not calling, was worse than not having seen him at all. As the afternoon darkened, the foggy feeling that had made everything so brilliantly clear, so perfect and fascinating, was lifting. I tried to tell myself that meeting my father again after ten years was a cause for celebration. I didn't remember his words, I remembered his face, the odd chuckle, the distance between what came out of his mouth and his expression.

After my uncle left in the late afternoon, and as the images of some Western presented themselves on the screen of the TV, shifting colors and shapes with no particular meaning, the sun went down completely, and the phone didn't ring.

I was a good student that semester, at least in the beginning, although I think I knew in the back of my mind I wouldn't return in the spring, even before I found out I was pregnant. To be pregnant wasn't a surprise, it was a vindication.

I thought something was growing in me from that early morning on the street, watching the nameless man walk in the other direction. Now I knew he had been real. I had embraced him and he had changed me. Manuel, who had been like my own brother, who watched me as I put the diaphragm in, couldn't make me pregnant. It took a man with a sickle, a man who squinted up at the sun like an angry orphan.

In letters to my mother, I told her about the department stores and matinees, not about Papa or the Bone Man. But I hoped, wished, wanted to believe she could understand the full feeling I had in my body, the weight of my shoes on the pavement.

I had bought a deck of tarot cards on the street one day, and from time to time I read them as one would a book. Once my uncle came into my room while I had them out.

"Are you going to follow in your mother's footsteps, Scarlett? You know things aren't the same."

Before I could answer, he sat down on the bed next to me and looked down at the cards. He touched one with his big, chubby hand and then withdrew his finger.

"Do you know what you're doing?" he asked.

"I'm just playing."

"You must be careful," he said, this time reaching his hand to my cheek. "The cards have power."

What did he know about the power of the cards, about the power surrounding his own plump hand, or the baby whiteness of his chest? He let power go, like sifted sugar through his fingers, or like a box of sparrows, flying willy-nilly in the backyard. Have you ever looked at a flock of birds and felt your own chest expand and contract with their flight pattern, as they soar in a close, slick line, and then scatter?

One night when Mercado was in a mood of bravado, condemning something or other, I stopped him in between bites of sausage and rice.

"You know, Uncle Mercado. I wanted to ask you something."

"Ask, baby. What are those cocksuckers thinking?" he said, shaking his fork at the television.

"What would it take to go into business for myself?"

"Business! You haven't even finished your first semester in school and you want to start your own business. That's the United States for you! Well done, Scarlettina."

"I'd like to read tarot cards."

"Uh-huh," he said, with an air of confusion.

"Tell fortunes," I continued.

"And what about school, Scarlett?"

"I want to go part-time, maybe, in the spring."

"But why? Why not stay in school? You've got financial aid, and the scholarship, and—"

"I'm also pregnant."

Mercado put down both his eating utensils, fork and knife, and leaned back abruptly in his chair.

"How could this happen?"

"The usual way, Uncle."

"I didn't even know you had a boyfriend. Can we look forward to—"

"No wedding, no boyfriend. It was an accident."

"Oh, Scarlett," he said, and got up from the table. He turned off the television set and looked at me.

I said, "I've seen the storefront fortune-tellers. It wouldn't cost much money to get started, and I was thinking—"

"Are you out of your mind? You are pregnant. A business! Fortune telling! No, impossible."

"But it's just a matter of putting up a sign and—"

"Ridiculous! Oh, how can a girl run a business? How can you, a child, imagine such things? You've gone wild already. This city has its dark side and it's gotten to you. You are so young, so young."

I looked down at the table.

"Oh, Scarlettina," he continued in a low voice, taking a big gulp of wine.

He scraped the floor with his chair, moving it over to my side of the table.

"You will always be my baby," he said thickly, putting his arm around me, placing his hand on my leg.

I felt confused after that and went to my room. I lay on my bed with only one little light on. In the other room I could hear Mercado laughing at some TV show after a while. He was drunk. Even later I heard what sounded like heavy furniture being moved, and then cursing, and then a vicious rattle. Then there was silence.

"Saint Clare," I whispered. But that's all I said.

I woke up early the next morning and went into the kitchen. The dishes from the night before were still undone, and in the dining room the table was bare. The salt and pepper shakers, an empty wine bottle, napkins and silverware were all jumbled up together in the tablecloth on the floor in the corner. The light was on. The

TV was on. I turned them off, and began taking things back into the kitchen and doing the dishes.

When my hands were pink and lined, the skin grainy and water-logged and smelling of both cleanser and black oven, Uncle Mercado emerged from his bedroom and came into the kitchen.

"You know a baby can't live here," he said, opening the refrigerator and pulling out a soda, then turning and going back to the rear of the apartment. I heard the steady stream of his urine in the toilet, even through the door, and then I heard his bedroom door close decisively, like a cruel sentence in the dark hall.

I opened for business on a cold, bright morning in December. It was Saint Clare, I thought, who led me to the tiny storefront with a bedroom in the back. One afternoon I was sorting through my papers when I came across a number Celia had given me, for her cousin. I went to visit Mary, and as soon as she saw me she said, "You have the look of a mother." I wasn't showing at all. I guess the supernatural was commonplace in her family, they were always finding twenty-dollar bills in teacups or consulting dead relatives on where to place the furniture. I told Mary what I wanted to do, and she squinted at me with her heavily made-up eyes and said she had to talk to her boyfriend, who owned a building and a car-service company in Queens. A week later I signed a handwritten agreement with him and had a place to live and work away from Uncle Mercado.

It was small, but on a main boulevard. I could only lay down flat in one direction on the floor in the front room, but the back room was about twice that size, and the one sink, which I used for brushing my teeth and doing dishes, had hot and cold running water. The windows were covered with old, yellowed newspaper, and the linoleum floor burped up in places where the tiles still existed at all. The Sheetrock walls in the front were unpainted, and creepy floral wallpaper covered the back room. Both rooms had overhead fluorescent lights, and there was a red bead door between them. I scrubbed the black grime off the walls and floor and put up Indian sheets I bought with some of the money my uncle gave me in guilty riddance. I tore the newspaper off the window and polished the glass with ammonia. In the middle of the window I put a neon light, a blinking eye Mary had found—some nightclub had ordered it and then went out of business. A blinking eye isn't exactly accurate for a fortune-teller, most have either the splayed, naked hand or the eye wide open as if in fright. But I liked this blinking light. The rim of the eye was a rich blue, a wild blue like the inside of a sea flower. The pupil was a sharp red curl that shut off when the eye blinked, and then reappeared.

My first customer was from Mary's boyfriend's car-service company next door. It was Rosa, the secretary there. She came in after the morning sun had left the front room and my coffee was stone cold. Rosa waved in front of the door. I unlocked it, and she said:

"Hello, I've come to have my fortune told. Isn't that fun? Mary told me all about you."

She breezed by me, rubbing her mittened hands together and smelling like hamburgers and french fries.

"What are your rates?"

I told her.

"Well, always help out a neighbor," she said, looking at her watch. "Anyway, I have twenty minutes left in my lunch hour."

I tried to smile.

She cut the cards at my request, giggling. I flipped over the first card from each pile: the Moon, the Five of Cups, the Four of Wands. Rosa seemed to be concentrating on the pictures.

"This card," I began, "represents your past. I see you had animals . . . a cocker spaniel, and another dog, brown and white, a—"

"Collie!" she interrupted.

"Yes, a collie. That was a happy home. There was a used car in the driveway, a broken car. No, the dog was broken, run over by that same blue Chrysler?"

She looked down and nodded.

"That dog and that home live on in your dreams. You visit them."

I saw a bleak smile cross over her face.

"Now you are a bit disappointed in things. The love in your life isn't going well. You miss a man. I see him, in the distance."

Her face was blank.

"This man, he is with you perhaps. But there is some element of distance . . . disappointment. Why are you sad, Rosa? Why do you turn away from the full cup?"

"I love him, but—" she said, straining.

"But you don't like his underpants."

She was taken aback.

"Certain physical things about him, personal choices, drive you away. You must decide, Rosa, what it means to attach so much importance to the small things, these repulsive little habits of his. If you love him, as you say, you must relinquish your hold on his shirt color, belt size, teeth rot. If you concentrate on them, you will lose the soul of the man you love."

She looked down, abashed.

"But Rosa, I see something bright in your future. I think you will be able to make such a choice and decide what is important. I see a couple turning away from the crowd and approaching a small structure . . . a house. . . . Yes, you will move out of the city."

"Oh, no!"

"Possibly?"

Rosa slapped her knee and laughed in delight.

"How can you know such things?" she asked gaily.

"*I* don't know anything, Rosa," I said, and tapped the cards with my finger.

✵

My mother wrote me at my uncle's address all that winter. I picked up the letters when I went to work at the pizzeria, which I kept doing while business got off the ground, which it did, but slowly, and as long as my belly was small enough to be safe from the lurch forward of the cash-register drawer, or the pizza maker's leaps and falls. Mama wrote on pink stationery, the kind made in France. I knew by writing me on that crisp, petal-like paper she was savoring the experience. The air mail sticker was a window of blue on the envelope. Her letters were carefully worded and concise. I knew they had been drafted at least once on the cheap, lined, newspaper-textured paper she had a pad of in the kitchen drawer. She asked me so carefully, "Do you like it there?" Someday I would tell her. But for now I wanted to let her imagine that school was better than the garden could ever be, that Uncle Mercado was a self-made millionaire, and that New York City was wooing me the old-fashioned way.

One April night, late into my pregnancy, I went outside on the street in front of my building and gazed at the low-lying buildings of Queens. I looked up, and the moon surprised me. I don't know what happened exactly, but something in my breast dissolved in that instant, like the clouds in the sky scattering. The Bone Man was separating out and losing his solidity. For a split second, I doubted him. I wasn't the little girl in the garden anymore, kneeling in front of the Saint Clare icon, placing the Death card gently and with precision by the rim of the birdbath. The taste of the nameless man was in my mouth, and he had been a stranger to me. He was the father of my child. The Bone Man hadn't come to me, he hadn't consummated his marriage to Saint Clare on the night my father lied to me about his love, I had simply slept with a human being. My hands pattered on my belly as I looked up and down the lonely street.

✳

I sat in the front room the next day holding a cup of coffee in my hand as I did every morning, watching the room shift almost unnoticeably in hue as the big blue eye winked and the red pupil flashed on and off. The week before I had set an extra set of cards on the windowsill, face up, so the pictures would tempt customers. Something about these cards bothered me that day, and I gathered them up again and put them away. While I was still in bed, I had felt the kicking of my baby. I had felt these movements many times before, but that morning the kick got me out of bed, it got me leaning on the counter trying to remember what I had forgotten, what had changed for me.

A man wearing a business suit, a raincoat and polished shoes came in, the most intellectual paper in the city stuffed under his arm like a teddy bear. He looked around at my room suspiciously. We discussed prices and options. His eyes were on my belly, and he looked from there to my face, as if wondering if a woman in my condition could, in fact, tell the future. When I asked him to cut the cards, he looked at me as if I'd told him to unzip his fly.

"I see a man in a field," I began, and I knew at the same time that his shoes were too small, and that he found this room unbearable. I knew my bare legs, akimbo from under my loose skirt, made him nervous. If he only knew the wisdom in his earlobe, which hears nothing at all.

"He is young, a boy in the first flush of manhood. He has paused in his work and looks over his shoulder. There is a dark, sinister figure at the edge of the forest. He is beckoning to the boy in the field. The boy puts down his shovel. He looks at the Queen Anne's lace and yarrow flowers. He traces one soft spiral, one slow explosion, with his hand. Then he looks up again. The man is still there, at the edge of the field, by the forest. What will the boy choose? The man in black? Or the intoxicating flowers?"

Beyond his puffy face, bloated from simple boredom, a flicker of life betrayed itself in the young man in front of me. Everyone has had this dream.

I looked down at the second card. I had my eyes focused on it, but I couldn't see the picture there. Was it the Six of Swords, the Ace of Cups, the Hierophant? I didn't know. But I spoke anyway.

"You are on a street corner, and the light has not turned green. You will stand here until you get a definite signal, a walk sign. That time has not yet come. You are choosing not to move forward. That is safe and sound."

He began to breathe easier. A chance for stagnation—that's what we're all looking for.

"See this crow here?" I indicated a bird in the left-hand corner of the middle card.

"Yes," he said, clearing his throat.

"It means you must not be obstinate. I don't need to tell you this, my friend."

I leaned back in my chair. He, or she, had kicked again. I felt like my mother and that was exasperating. She took to telling the future because she had looked at all the conventional signs and hadn't seen what she needed to see. As a girl, she had a dream, and that dream led her down the aisle with a man who promised such things, promised them not so much in his words, though there was that, but in his eyes, in the twinkle that said: possibility. Everything was in those eyes: she jumped into them as if she were jumping into the fragrant air, flying around unaccountably. Why was I here?

I looked down at the third card, the future. Again, a cloud passed over the picture on the table. I was left with my own memory.

"I see a young girl in a garden. She is slowly, carefully picking weeds. There is a man and a woman in the near vicinity. They smile at each other. He swept her off her feet. He carried her over the threshold into a world of dream. The little girl looks up and drops the clump of weeds."

I stopped and looked into the blue and red eye, blinking.

"What does that mean?" the man asked, and his voice came from far, far away. A man and a woman can sit across from each other at a table where the past, present and future are laid out like silverware, and they can eat. This man wanted to know something. He wanted me to tell him about the future, so he could rest easy. I looked back into his sad, real eyes, and I had nothing to say.

The Dove

H ave you ever met a man who is an invocation, as rich and
sensuous as still-wet oil paint on a field of battle? Have you
ever rubbed up against a person and come away smudged and liquid with the testy perfume of the oils, the fantastically hopeful
raw material? At a distance he may have looked like another man,
his red coat, after all, looked real, his teeth gleamed white and
pale. But if you got closer, and closer still, if you let your hand fall
toward his lapel, then you'd see the brush strokes on his sleeve.
You could rub your cheek against his and come away black,
green, vermilion.

Centina met a man like this, a week before her wedding.

The bartender leans over the bar. He tells the customers: "She's
been at the hotel for months. When her husband died, she sold all
their furniture and moved here."

Centina sits by the fire. Her Brandy Alexander has separated
and warmed in the glass before her. The beads on her black che-
mise glimmer. She watches the door.

It was at the funeral parlor itself that Centina wrote the first letter. So many hours, you know. Nothing to do. She had been following him through the international newspapers, through military
journals. He was a hero. A hero to one cause, a traitor to another.

58

Her black-gloved hand scribbled out the address of the hotel.

She did it as a last act of free will, a gesture. She flew across the ocean and let her mother handle the bridesmaids' last-minute questions, the tablecloth colors; anyway, it seemed as much a wedding for her parents as for herself: the capturing of a good doctor. In Spain, she ate yellow candy, lemon slices made of jelly and crispy with sugar. Her future was a mountain before her. A cup of strong black tea cooled on the marble table. Small brown birds, the color of doll's hair, fretted on the terrace and in the bushes. Beyond the bushes, beyond the mountain, was a wilderness. She felt the call, the approach of danger. Was there anything so venomous and ill-intentioned as the cat behind her breastbone, the creature heaving inside her? Centina's flesh tingled. She ate the yellow slices out of the wrappers and licked her fingers.

Penny is brushing her hair in the bathroom. Her mother is downstairs doing a hundred things. The house smells of Saturday morning: lemon-scented furniture polish, waffles, tomorrow's spaghetti sauce on the stove. Her little sister knocks impatiently at the door. But Penny doesn't hear her, she isn't thinking of her family, or of cooking or cleaning. She's listening to the fluttery music of her Aunt Centina's wedding, fifteen years before, when she was just a little girl. Centina threw the bouquet to Penny, her flower girl. Centina's eyes glittered with love for Uncle Oliver. Now Penny is planning her own wedding. It is her turn to be the woman drowning in a pool of infectious white flowers.

Penny can barely hold back her tears when she thinks of Centina's sorrow, she can't imagine a loss so severe.

If you knew she was drunk, would it matter? That they sat on the rock, and he convinced her to throw her jewelry, piece by piece, into the water? First the watch (because time is easy to attack), then the string of pearls (she ripped it apart, sending the white beads all over), then each ring (including the diamond cluster), and last, the precious heirloom choker. One by one, the jewels fell into the slowly rippling water. At the height of their arc they glittered, then splashed, white and black, gone forever. Little sparkling reminders, lifting and falling like lucky pennies, lost desires.

When she was naked and black in the patchy moonlight, he wrapped himself around her, soft as a sedative, soothing her, stroking her, until she fell into a swoon, a torpor. The stone underneath felt soft as clay, he was a furry shadow inside her. The ice-cracked sky shook, and the scream of recognition she let go was small and sharp and forever.

But that is over now. Centina sits carefully on a chair in her hotel room, as if no longer the same animal. She is in the middle of the book today. She chuckles at the same parts as last time around. She makes notes in the margins, the same notes as she made yesterday, new letters over old.

It was about the book that they struggled on the road, about the book that she skinned her palms and his nose bloodied. It was about the book, dried around his lips and forehead, that she tasted the metallic fruit of his insensibility, the orange crust of his rage. The words are the crusts now, his features etched on the page. She remembers, but she has forgotten, so she reads. She reads and reads and reads. Pieces of sentences, she holds onto, bits of a blown-up canvas, blown to smithereens.

The phone rings.

"You have a visitor," the doorman says into the receiver.

Centina hangs up. It has to be.

She stands at the first landing, her hands clutching the banister. She is dressed in a red suit. Her ash blonde hair is curled under. From the lobby she looks thirty-five or forty, but Penny knows she is older. Her mouth opens, and closes again. Her words, if they came, would be rose petals. The blood in her veins, if she has any, would be lavender. She opens and closes her mouth and what comes out? No words, no sound. She leans forward as if she might collapse, or bound off like an acrobat to the floor.

Penny mounts the stairs. Centina backs up, her shoulder pressing against the wall.

"Hello, Aunt Centina! It's been so long. I'm sorry to bother you, I know you're in mourning and all. . . ."

Her aunt turns and lurches down the hall to her room, locking the door behind her.

Penny weeps outside the hotel; the doorman studiously looks away from her. Death is such an atmosphere. It's breathtaking how long it lasts, how stricken with love is her Aunt Centina. Penny shocks herself with pictures of her fiancé dead and immobile, herself flitting around the body. What would she do without him? Her heart would simply stop beating. She closes her eyes and imagines a white beam of light, an understanding, between herself and the woman in the hotel.

Centina strips. She remembers stripping. She takes off everything: her shoes, her stockings, her bra, her pearls. She lies down on the bed and curls up, the pillows all around her in a wall. She has left her clothes in a mess on the chair. The book lies on the table. She opens one eye and sees it. She winds up her leg and kicks it with a fury to the floor.

In the evening the bartender wonders what has happened to Centina. She's become a source of entertainment for the regulars: an heiress in mourning, a vacant stare. But tonight she isn't in the bar.

Upstairs the French windows are open, the wind blows into Centina's room. She stands at the window, the November air rushing through her lovely robe, pulling the curl from her hair. On the ledge, the pigeons chuckle and shuffle their feathers.

✵

His medals, thick and clustered, fell brilliantly from his collar. He threw his jacket around her after they swam in the water. The medals nearly crushed Centina. She bit at them and tugged them with her fingers.

The flower girl turned bride-to-be returns the next morning. Again, the phone rings. This time Centina answers it without lunging across the room. She simply shrugs her shoulders and says yes, let Penny come.

Centina sits in a chair. She is dressed in black, not a stitch out of order. Penny thinks perhaps she is going to visit the cemetery to bring Oliver flowers. She nervously holds the cream-colored envelope.

"Hello, Aunt Centina. I won't be long. But I wanted to tell you that I'm getting married. On February second, only a couple of months from now. You see, I've always remembered your wedding. It is an example for me. You were the perfect bride. I was just hoping you could be at our ceremony."

She extends her arm, as if to give Centina the invitation. Centina doesn't move. Penny understands. She will put it on the table instead. But when she's placing it there, she sees a picture, a photograph. It's not of Uncle Oliver. It's a general, an army man. He's dark and foreign.

Still clutching the envelope, Penny looks back at Centina.

"Are you going to the cemetery?"

"The cemetery? No."

"Who's that man?"

"Handsome, isn't he?" Centina says, her lips twisting into a half-smile.

Penny's heart quickens, she drops the invitation on the table.

✶

After Penny leaves, Centina stays seated for a moment, and then she rises. She looks in the mirror to check her lipstick, her teeth, her hair. The envelope sits quietly on the table, by the book, by the picture. Her hand reaches toward it, but falls on the book instead. She holds this to her breast and walks toward the open window.

He rode a Lippizaner. His boots hugged the horse's swelling white body with quiet power. The animal's thick neck arched, shoulders quivered. It stepped in formation, steaming under saddle.

Penny squints at the sunshine outdoors. It is a beautiful day, so perfect there are no shadows. Soon, her head will be covered in a veil, her arms draped in satin. Who is that man in Aunt Centina's photograph, and what does it matter? Penny's husband will undo all hundred and twelve silk-covered buttons, Penny's hands will hold the flowers.

In the corner of her eye, Penny sees a blackbird, falling.

Out of the sky, falling like stars, comes her jewelry. It is he who is beside her. She feels his breath heavy and sweet in the velvet air. She will free him of his medals this time.

Centina's teeth shatter.

How to Have a Broken Heart

First, you must believe in the heart. The heart is a leaf off a small tree among other trees. The heart-leaf is red, the red of breathing. In a dream you let your hand wander up the side of your body and touch the smooth edge of the leaf. You are drawn in by a perfume you don't understand. You have a moment when you seem to have choice, when your intellect works, when you assess things—lifestyle, hairstyle, hands, accoutrements. These moments are fine and delicate, and you deceive yourself in leaps and bounds. You remember things—you have associations. He reminds you of your first boyfriend. You believe you will be able to resist him. You see everything in a glance. You see cruelty approaching. You seize it and believe you have conquered the cruelty, but instead you have the heart in your hand. You took the heart-leaf off the tree in that momentary confidence, and instead of saving yourself from the blistering cruelty, you let it in. It had been so clear to you that you were going to resist. You were aware of the danger, fully and utterly, because you saw the bearlike hands pouring the baby wine, you saw how the delicate glass looked between those fingers, you saw how the lips moved to receive the wine. And then there was the suitcase. A small affair— smaller than you would take for a trip. You would take everything with you given a chance. There was wind in the suitcase. There was a small pile of smoothed-down heart-leaves, still moist from the tree. The leaves were slipped in between socks and razors, between coming and going, between appearance and dislocation. *It's not love,* you say to yourself in hopeless lament. But when you try to repeat the line, to further convince yourself, even these words can't be spoken. You have been taken in. The raw leaf feels smooth and you trail your fingers like a blind person over the sharpness of the edge. Each side is the same blue-red—in your blind grope you search for imperfection in the color, but it is pure and unalloyed. Yes, you say, eyes closed, this feels like blue, I can feel the temptation here, I can see a distance with clarity, I can see the sky, I can see the changing of the seasons, I can see the inside of a stone here. I know it is red, too, you say to yourself, breathing in, feeling the solidity of this color. So you have the leaf in your hand now. You are responsible for it. You have the impression your eyes are open, but you keep trying to open them. Now you have your eyes focused on the leaf, and you are trying to make the leaf out, but the fine-pointed edges have extended into the five digits of your own hand, the leaf has pressed itself into your skin like a gravestone rubbing, it has curled around the fleshy part of your thumb like a warm, insinuating friend. You take your other hand and you try to pick it off a little on the sides. But the edge is too thin, it's like peeling plastic wrap: you think you've got it, but you haven't. You hold up your hand and squint, shaking your head, trying to focus and refocus on this. Have you ever had a dream in which you can't open your eyes? In this situation you can't close them. But what you see doesn't seem real or natural, so you keep blinking.

The next step? You put your hand in your pocket and try to walk down the street as if nothing has happened. This makes you feel a little self-conscious, and you can barely mutter hello at the passing people in the street, friends, business associates, old lovers. Mostly you keep your mouth closed and try to keep them at bay with clipped sentences. You go to the hardware store to pick up some paint—you think you will paint something. You have this nervous vision. You think holding a brush in the hand will give it something to do besides move toward the object, the man. So you go to the hardware store and you pick out a fluttery dropcloth which you will paint on, and you get some clothespins which you will hang the dropcloth from, and you stand, hands under your arms, in front of the paint selection. You have no notion of color, except for the blue-red feeling. But the colors all lined up here on the shelf with names like Blue Whisper sicken you, they are an atrocity when it comes to the live color in your hand. You pick white. You will paint on a white background. You will paint in your backyard, with the radio on. You bring your selections to the counter and act casual and nonchalant as you wait in line; you steal glances at the man behind the counter, you think he is a policeman. You are impatient with the woman in front of you, counting her change and asking pointed questions about roofing. You envy her concern with tiles. You wonder what it would be like to take advice in so smooth a fashion. When you stand in front of the cash register, you have your sleeve pulled over your hand as if it is missing, like handless people put their empty-space hand in their pockets and pretend. You make some excuse that was not asked for. You blurt out, "It happened by accident," and the man behind the register looks at you blankly, and you try to explain again, and then you see the letters F-A-N-T-A-S-Y spelled in those cop eyes of his, and you shut up and take your packages with you to your backyard where you intend to use them. But then you realize you are hungry, and you go to the kitchen to make a sandwich, but the red of the heart-leaf-hand smears on your bread and so even this nice peanut-butter sandwich looks unappetizing. You go to the bathroom to brush your teeth, and when you rinse out your mouth the whole sink is bloody with that distinct/indistinct flavor/smell that you recognized and didn't recognize at the tree itself, and which speaks to you alone. So you run the tap water for a long time.

By the time you return to your backyard it is twilight. You look up at the places the stars will be and you have a litany of crass thoughts and cheap emotions. The big white sheet looks appalling, rustling in the wind like a nervous dog. But you put the jar down on the ground anyway and you've taken the cap off. You stand there with your arms folded and you can't see the red trailing from under your arm, down the side of your body, to the ground. You watch the way the sheet becomes phosphorescent as the moon comes up. The sheet begins to hum with the blueness behind the red. The corner flaps up and you are unaccountably startled. It flaps up gently and then slaps down. You try to secure the edge with a stone.

The paint goes on easily and you keep dabbing at it for a while, intent on a certain section. Where you touch the sheet with the white paint, it is opaque, so you are drawing opaque lines in a field of moonlight. You dab together what looks like a leaf, a heart, a hand. It takes a long time. You trace it larger then smaller then larger again. By the time you are finished, the whole sheet is wet and stiff with paint, and you can't see the moon in it anymore. When you step back to admire your work—not that you are in the frame of mind to admire anything—when you step back to at least see what you've done, you see that the sheet does not shine, does not flap, does not show signs of a new answer. But you hesitate to take it down. You turn around and go upstairs to your room and go to bed. In bed, it's as if the bleeding has slowed down. You go the whole night and there is only a little stain on the right-hand side of the bedcovers. When you wake up in the morning, your hand feels swollen.

Perhaps it's time to meet the loved one again. And so the phone rings, and when you answer it your palm is wet and red, and the phone nearly slips, but you say yes to a certain meeting at a certain time. You dress your hand up. You put a bracelet on. The hand still looks a bit raw and it's impossible to hide, really. The bracelet looks garish. You take the bracelet off, you twist the ring off your finger, but then you put it on again. The hand throbs and you look at it and feel afraid. You don't recognize it. It looks like your hand, like your life, but it is not. It is something else. Yet it masquerades as your hand. You had, as an experiment, let your hand be seen in public at a party, and no one seemed to notice anything different. They all thought it was the same old you and the same old hand. This is a bit confusing, but you know you're living with a leaf in your hand.

On the way to the meeting your hand is in your lap and it rests there, waiting. You imagine that it wants to clasp another hand, his hand, because hands come in pairs like that. Your own other hand isn't up to the task. It, your left hand, is the misfit, and it simply keeps things going where it can—it tries to feed you, pay the bills, keep up appearances. You feel a bit lopsided with a mismatched pair of hands. You have an instinct for balance, and you believe the man has the other hand in the pair. You believe in the balance of two hands. You are a little desperate about it. It seems like the only way to heal your own hand. When you imagine the coming union, meeting, matching of hands, you feel very light, except for the weight in your right hand.

Then you are with the man again. There he is, by the tree where the leaf was. You come up to him, a bit bashful about your lumpy hand, listing a little to one side. You keep the hand behind your back. You want to show it immediately, but you are afraid. You and the man have a glass of wine together. In the redness of the wine you become temporarily lost, reminded of the redness of the hand and the heart and the leaf. The smoke around your head creates a distance you mistake for the mysterious blue feeling. Slowly, as the red wine stains your lips and throat and body with the same color as your hand, you bring the hand out and let it rest on the bar between you and the man. You think perhaps it will meld with the color of the wine and the blue cigarette smoke. But when he looks down at the raw hand, he doesn't recognize it. Now you realize you are actually hugely disappointed. You wanted it to blend in because you were afraid. Really you want it to be noticed. You say something like, "Do you see the ring on my finger?" hoping to draw attention to the strange flowering hand. He sees the ring on your finger, but he doesn't see the hand. He covers your hand with his own clean white one. You are alarmed. Your hand flips over in a last-ditch effort. But the redness of your hand doesn't stain his, and the white coldness of his hand just makes yours burn.

The Roller Skating Queen

Anna puts on her reading glasses and squints at the chemistry table. Her fingers, tipped with red, vampish nails, drum on the book's side. There is interference on the radio, soiling a sexy song.

She has an hour before she must dress for work. In less than that, her son will wake, and her mother will wake, too. It is raining outdoors and Jamie's galoshes smile at the toes where the rubber has split. It is raining outdoors and Anna's mother has just been left by her boyfriend for the third or fourth time. The family has yet to discover he took with him her old wedding band.

In a coffee can in the kitchen cabinet, some dollars and change are hidden away, and, perhaps a sentimentalist, the boyfriend did not take them, as well. The can is called the Good Wish Can, and Anna, Carla and Jamie take money from it sometimes to buy something special: cheddar cheese popcorn, two pints of rich ice cream, a taxi drive through Central Park. Anna puts what she can of her paycheck in the Good Wish Can at the end of the week. There is twenty-one dollars in it now.

Even with her ugly, teacher glasses on, Anna can't focus on the numbers and letters and equations that make up a formula, a law, the inherent property of things. If she could just *focus*, see the words, things might be different. She could force herself to plow through the pages. As it is she forgets one sentence to the next. She confuses an equal sign with a not-equal sign, the symbol for infinity with a degree.

Anna feels two big hot hands on her shoulders; her mother is bending down to kiss her cheek near the ear.

"Hello darlin'," her mother murmurs, and then turns toward the coffee maker. Anna takes off her glasses and watches her mother's lumbering, bearlike body reach for the filters, stretching until her pink velour robe lifts above her knees.

Anna goes into her room and looks at her son. He is lying in the middle of a whirlwind of lap blankets, disengaged fitted sheets and cushions. His cartoon-figured pajamas are wrapped around his legs and torso so tightly it's surprising he doesn't lose circulation. Nonetheless, he snores (or snorts) regularly in a deep sleep.

"Time to get up," she whispers, leaning over him on the thin mattress, kissing his cheek, his temple, his hand. He sleeps too much, too deeply, for a five year old. He sleeps like a dead man.

The boyfriend has left before, and each time Anna lets out a sigh as long and bitter as gooseberry branches. This morning she paces to the bathroom, clumsily bewitching the house, exorcising him once again. With him gone, the short hallway that serves as the starship belly for this tiny apartment grows taller and fatter, the walls soar up another one or two feet on all sides.

In front of the bathroom mirror, Anna strips and throws her arms up in the air. She peers at her splayed image.

Two months ago she found the body of the family poodle in this very room, his mouth wide and stiff like a clasp-pocketbook that's been gutted. She never noticed how dull and pathetic his brown-orange curls were until that morning. Now Jamie wants a new dog. A Doberman, like his friend Steven's.

She steps into the trickling shower and imagines she's the queen of Madagascar.

71

✳

On days like this the Circle Line attracts no one, but they still keep the ferry's engine chugging balefully in the harbor. Anna stares out of the ticket window and chews the slice of coffee cake that the secretary brought for her. The rain falls in patterns, it sweeps across the nearly empty parking lot. The gray water in the harbor is rising with all the rain. Anna thinks of it behind her, sloshing in big bucketfuls over the rim of the earth. She imagines a flood that will carry away the illegally parked cars, drown the whores who sometimes wander, as if lost, in her direction.

The animal shelter reception area is filled with pictures of fluffy kittens playing with string next to mangled and starved versions of the same kind of animal. The place is green, the green of pain, and Anna's nostrils fill with the piercing smell. One wall is covered with cages. From each cage eyes follow her.

The high school volunteer is a guard, not an animal lover. She leads Anna into the dog chamber. The dogs look up, feet politely placed in front of them, as if they were frozen in time, remembering a day in the park, waiting to catch a ball.

Anna has barely gotten out the door to the hall when she looks smack into the burning eyes of a black cat, its shoulders and haunches sharp as knives under the skin.

"How long does this one have?" she inquires.

The girl looks at her strangely. Death is unspoken here. Anna turns and heads back to the reception area.

"I'll take it," she says.

The girl said she can pick up the cat tomorrow. Standing at the bus stop, Anna smiles a screwed-up smile. Has she gone crazy? She marched into the animal shelter looking for an attack dog and came out with nothing but a promise for a cut of old velvet wrapped around a hanger. Anna swings her pocketbook reck-lessly, as if daring someone to stop her.

Jamie was conceived under a full moon, during a fiesta. At that particular party everyone, including children, drank sips of tequila out of thimble-size plastic cups. Old mothers who were demure and rugged during the day let out their belts and sang love songs. Men crawled around on their hands and knees, picking up women's shoes in their teeth. In the kitchen, half a dozen families' crockery dishes lay empty after a frenzied eating. Anna's mother, in particular, was the life of the party. She spent the last part of the evening holding court in one fat chair, quietly laughing.

Anna bends down and ties her skates at the ankles. She has put the rice on the stove, watched it come to a boil like an absurdly slow heartbeat catching fire. In the living room her mother and Jamie shriek at the TV, vicariously playing a game show. He had a per-functory hug for her, and a shrug of the shoulders concerning school. Her mother was all aglitter, so without asking Anna knew Lance was coming back. In a short moment of lucidity, or panic, Anna realized she had a few minutes of freedom, on the pretext of fetching an onion or two.

She bumps down the flight of stairs. It was impetuous, stupid really, to put on her skates inside, but she wanted to wear them as long as possible: two bulky wings, cumbersome, used, gray as an incinerator.

When she returns, the rice is black at the bottom and the game show is over. Lance is sitting on the couch, his arms stretched over the boy and his old girl. Anna takes Jamie's hand roughly and pulls him away.

"Get your hands off him," she mutters.

"The bitch on wheels is back. How 'bout a kiss for Uncle?"

"Go fuck yourself."

"Anna!"

Her mother's look of prom queen innocence reaches Anna, makes her choke down a sob.

"I'm sorry, Mama. Dinner will be ready in about five."

"All sass, your little girl. Someday I'm going to kick her butt."

The tall man pads after Anna into the kitchen. He opens the refrigerator and pulls out a beer.

"You ought to treat your mother with more respect."

She can feel him watching her and hear him sniffling and sipping the beer. When she reaches around for the potholder they look at each other. He puckers his lips. Her legs and arms crumble.

The night of Jamie's conception Anna's mother looked like a radiant goddess from another country, another time. She wore a dress from Mexico, a white flowing beauty with brilliant embroidered roses and blue tears and green winding vines. At her breast, a yellow sun trembled with each dance step. No one could have resisted her that night, but Lance was a particular man. Fastidious and dark when it came to her appearance, he chastised Carla for gaining weight, slapped her cheek if he spotted another fine age line. She sought to please him with the teeming goodwill of a child. She giggled anxiously when he arrived that night, drunk, scanning the room with his handsome eyes.

Anna was in the kitchen, cleaning up a bit. She was, in a few years, going to be a chemist, or a pharmacist in a drug store. At school she gazed up at the huge chart in the science lab and read the secret language, giddy at the whispered message. And so, while listening to the grown-ups riot in the next room, she poured beer on angel food cake, hard cider into Parmesan cheese. She subjected lemon rinds to extremes of temperature, flung raspberries into cola.

"How old are you?" Anna heard from behind, as she measured a tablespoon of bleach into the maraschino cherry jar.

She looked around. Lance was chewing ice, squinting at her with his head held appraisingly to one side.

"Seventeen."

"You look older."

She didn't answer.

"Do you have a boyfriend?"

"What?"

"Do you have a boyfriend who carries your books for you? Helps you out of your uniform?"

"I've got to do the dishes now."

He walked toward her and she poured the cherry experiment down the sink. He put his hand on her bottom.

"Mmmm."

"Stop that."

"What's in here?" he asked, pointing to a door.

"I don't know," Anna lied.

"Let's find out."

It was the entrance to the back hall, to the garbage chute, to the windowless tunnel of a lifetime, lost in a moment of unfair gravity, disastrous chemical proportions.

It is Saturday. Anna and Jamie are going to Central Park. Jamie wants to watch the softball games that run up and down the Great Lawn. In a couple of years he'll be old enough for Little League, and he holds onto that possibility as if it were the most important thing in the world.

When they get to the baseball diamond, Jamie asks Anna if she would let him sit there by himself for a while. He is embarrassed, bored by his mother. She stares at him for a blank moment. In another thirteen years, she reasons, he will be an adult. But she is almost certain, with a vague sense of relief, that she will lose him long before then.

"Sure," she says.

It would have been a fine day for roller skating, but Jamie is demoniacally jealous of this activity. Anna left her skates at home.

Anna walks toward the open spaces, the pavement anyway. She spots a little derby. A dozen skaters are swirling in time to a tin-can radio. As she nears them she gulps the heady wind. An old man in a purple leotard and a wispy scarf pirouettes in the context of the circle. Big brilliant bodies lunge forward, Santa Claus eyes winking at teenage girls in the crowd. Women rush along, running on skates, looks of abandon and fervor on their faces. And no children—

Anna drops Jamie off with her mother. She goes back out, taking the twenty-one dollars with her. It's a wildly sunny day for April. She imagines the cat blinking.

"May I help you?" the same girl at the desk asks, gazing up at her with turtle eyes.

"I was here yesterday, remember? I'm here for the cat we saw in the hall."

She doesn't seem to recall. She asks for Anna's name, unearths her application papers.

"We can go back and see if he's still here."

He is not in the green room. He is not in the hall. The girl checks in the back, leaving Anna with her back to the window.

When she returns, the girl says: "Sorry, he's gone. Did you want another?"

"Gone? What do you mean?"

"We can't keep cats forever."

"Did someone take him, or—"

"How do I know?" the girl counters.

Anna skates, weaving through the people. The street is paved with holiday sparklers, a million diamonds she could get to if she knelt down and scraped them up with her fingers. She pushes her weight down hard on physical matter.

✻

Back on the couch with her son and mother, Anna watches the game show. She sinks into the natty yellow cushions, the color of an ill old man, with burnt orange foam squeezing out from the corners. She hurrahs when Jamie gets the right answer, but the hum of laughter is far away, like the surface of water. The louder they scream and the more frequent their laughter, the further she is from the air.

In the booth, Anna plans a new wardrobe. She creates outfits that she knows she could never buy. She gives particular care to the details of her new dresses, slippers, coats; she nearly falls asleep in a dream of organdy and silk, wool and leather.

Again, Anna counts the years until Jamie will be a grown man, until all his pajamas and miniature toothbrushes will have gone, disappeared.

Tonight after work she will go to her class at the university, Chemistry 2. It is her last prerequisite before pharmaceutical science. In a year and a half, she'll have her degree. She'll find a good job and begin to pay off her student loans. In ten years that will be over. Then she can save some money to go on vacation. To the Bahamas. She'll take a week or maybe even two weeks, and go there, with bright, flustered new bathing suits, high-heeled sandals and matching luggage.

The sun flings itself in short, ugly leaps onto the hoods of cars. Anna has never known the sun to be as selfish as it is here. She lets her eyes trail the slowly replaced cars, people.

At the black magic store she trails her hands over the amulets, oils, rocks and charms. A fabulously pale woman points her eyes at her. Anna remembers, as a little girl, her mother rocking her, and keeping her sweater from falling off her shoulders. She leaves with a packet of get-away powder, made with wisteria. If you

77

want to rid the atmosphere of spiritual pests, the woman said, dust it around your door.

Her mother baked cookies and cakes all day today, while Anna was at work and school and at the store. When she gets home Jamie's olive-colored face is patched with melted chocolate and butter.

"Mom! Nana made cookies!" he says. Anna is glad. She sits next to her son on the damp yellow couch and looks at his facial structure. How much longer can her mother go without seeing it? Could she believe that every love object just naturally resembles the other?

"Anna, darling," her mother says, arms outstretched, apron filthy with flour. Anna lets Carla hug her, flour and all.

"You must be tired, sweetheart. Do you want cookies and milk? A beer?"

"I'm OK, Mama."

Anna fingers the powder in her pocket. She is too far away to be a mother. Jamie is showing her a tracing he did of a Lamborghini. It is uncentered on the page, aiming downward to the bottom right-hand corner. His pencil markings are thin but somehow sure. She is appalled.

"Can we save up to buy one?" he asks.

"I don't think so."

"Why not?"

"I don't know."

"When can we get a dog, Mommy?"

"What do you want a dog for?"

"To protect us from robbers."

"It's safe here. We don't need a dog."

"Liar!"

"Watch your mouth."

"You're a real bitch, y'know?"

His face is twisted into a disgusted scowl. Anna's red-tipped hand slaps it. He feels like stone to her.

"Shut up! Have some respect!"

Lance is helping her mother out of the pink robe when Anna returns later. Her mother is giggling. It is dark except for the TV. Jamie, she guesses, is in her room.

Anna lets her skates drop to the floor on her way to the kitchen. She pours herself a glass of water and sits down at the table, flipping to the correct page in her textbook.

The periodic table stares out at her.

She heard Jamie—she means Lance—say things to her as she walked through the living room. She realizes this only now.

She drinks her water methodically, trying to decipher the taste. What is nothing? What does it consist of exactly? As a chemist, she should know.

She takes a second glass of water to bed. Jamie is sleeping. She likes him asleep, his face softened into that of a real child. She quietly unsnaps her bra, pulls down her underpants—all the while keeping her eyes fixed on Jamie's face, afraid he will grow older.

Anna unties the string on the packet by the light of the street. She has never considered using a potion before. But if chlorine and ammonia can make a gas, why couldn't elements hold other, more secret, powers? Once she might have been wary of such things, but tonight she is impatient, that's all.

Anna tiptoes into the hall. Her mother and Lance have gone to bed, their door is closed. She dips her hand into the bag of powder, all she could buy with twenty-one dollars. "Get away," she whispers, sprinkling it on the door to her mother's bedroom, the way her mother sprinkles sugar. Anna listens for a minute. She thinks she hears a leg falling, a body rising to meet another. She frowns, and creeps to the front door. "Get away," she whispers again, scattering a trail on the floor. She listens for a sound, but hears nothing.

Anna walks over to the couch and sits down, the bag clutched in her hand. Like a starved person, she brings a handful of wisteria to her mouth and licks it, then another handful, and then another—

The yellow powder sits on her tongue and then explodes. Her belly contracts as she swallows, her skin becomes wet and cold. She endures these reactions with scientific calm. When the nausea passes and the spinning slows down, Anna opens her eyes. All is quiet in the small apartment. The lights from the street shine in thick, shadowy columns across the couch. In the corner, her roller skates give off a smug glow.

Belle's Sister

The dining room was empty and still when I looked down, and when I looked back up, there she was, reading, at the first table by the door.

"May I help you?"

"Just a coffee for now."

Beatrice is eating ice cream in the back, out of the five-gallon container. Why can't she bother fixing the coffee in advance just once, I wonder. She knows it's supposed to be on by five. Tapping my sneaker on the tile, I take a look around the corner. That woman, she reminds me of someone, and the space between my shoulders stiffens like a bone.

Out the window I watch car lights blur and streak on the sleek black pavement. The rain has made it darker than usual at this hour. With a fever I long to be outside, in a car, going somewhere, anywhere. Beatrice has turned the lights on low, and now she's lighting the candles on each table. I see her move in the glass. I see the little match flicker. And there's the customer, she's a brilliant reflection, all dressed in white. She's wearing a white wool skirt and white silk over her shoulders. I don't think she's come from work. She's not meeting anyone either. No, she's not ruffled, and she didn't protest when I took away the second set of silver.

Perhaps she's on a trip, outside a cab is waiting, and in the trunk she has a hatbox and a suitcase with a wide leather strap.

"Miss? I'd like to order."

Her face is perfectly round. It's taut as a melon: eyes, nose and mouth chiseled into stone. Around the edges of her brown eyes I notice a haze, a misting. We could be sisters together.

"I'd like the chicken Florentine. Does that come with a salad?"

"Yes."

"All right then, I'll have the house dressing."

She hands me the menu.

"Is that all?"

"Yes, that's all."

She's an aristocrat, her hair sweeps up in a wheat-colored wave. I waltz back to the kitchen with a brisk, graceful step. Only a waitress knows how to dance when her heart stops.

I will fill her glass with water. Serve from the left. Won't leave the garnish under the warmer. I will fill the saltshaker and add extra sugar. After all, I have a job to do, whether it's mopping up behind the counter or carving a sculpture. I have my own things to attend to. In another two months I'll have gotten my credit-card balance down to zero, and by August the car payments will be over. But she, she's a playwright, I'm sure. Famous and fearless in style. Writing every morning on a glass table on the porch, with wrought-iron legs and a teacup in the corner.

"Belle, you're up."

I will fill her glass with water.

In the morning I sit at the kitchen table, all hunched over. In her bedroom my adoptive mother is already calling. She carries on a conversation through the wall. With a napkin I slowly wipe my crumbs into a pile.

"It's time to change Dad's flowers. Did you hear me? I said it's time to—"

"I heard you."

"I think chrysanthemums would be nice this week. A nice big bunch. Do you think?"

Her voice is a rasping in the cool, close air.

This is what I'm dreaming. Matilda—so I've named her—and I are on the terrace after a long rain. Now the sun is coming, but it's the end of the day, a white fog fills the air. The tree limbs emerge from nowhere with urgent new messages. When I close my eyes I see raindrops hanging loosely from every pine needle. She has a secret, I know. We stare ahead. And I know there is a great danger. Beside me she sits, I cannot look at her, I do not know what I will see. I sit in the chair, watching the fog lift and the night come down around me.

Mother tells me he was a good man and I believe her. At the florist the woman behind the counter puts out her cigarette fast as if I'll be torn up inside if I see anything that reminds me of cancer. But I was already an orphan. I don't care.

All day long I've had a bird in my stomach. I pin the gas pedal to the floor. The car moves ahead fitfully. Yellow chrysanthemums rot on the passenger seat and black wings flap in my belly. I try to remain calm. I make plans, look ahead: I have the laundry, Mother's bedsheets, to consider.

I'll tell you a little story. Inside me the wind curls and howls in the spaces between my bones. I always think of the house, the house abandoned, cobwebbing up the stairs, frayed tablecloth, wind chimes still. When I was little I went to a baseball game with the man who called himself my father. I expected a home run. My friend had told me that hot dogs were ground-up cats, so I didn't eat any. All afternoon I watched the space above the people, thinking that home run ball would fly in my direction.

It started with the house. In an empty ballroom, dust on the windows, late afternoon light, a pinafored girl stepped lightly on parquet. There are springs underneath the wooden planks, they told her, so the bride's feet won't get tired. The girl placed her feet in circles and swung her empty arms around the world.

The Saint Mary's gate clicks behind me with fastidious pride and the golf course lawn and picnic table gravestones reel ahead. I plod forward.

She has wings. What I mean to say is, Matilda is taking flying lessons. She uses one of those old caps and wears boots like riding boots and a belt strapped around her waist. She's flying a Cessna now. Her pilot friend, the instructor, asked her on a date. She dipped, and swung around.

She wore white. Over and over I smooth my palms against the white cotton napkins, folding them into clumsy swans. Beatrice sits beside me, chatting. I can't move too quickly. The napkins gleam in my lap. The restaurant is dark, the lights are turned down. I smooth the napkins over and over again. I run my fingers along the edges. I lay my hands down: the gleam is overwhelming.

"Where are you going?" Beatrice asks, as I run toward the door.

They are stolen every time. Is it minutes after I throw them down, or hours? Do they get shuttled over to another grave, or are they delivered with wet naked hugs to a lover? What would Mother say if I told her?

Digging my fingernails into the hot wooden gate on the pier, I watch the ferry fill up with halves of couples, long lost uncles, mothers and fathers. I have so little time. Out of the crowd a figure emerges, soft and bright against the March sky.

✳

"Belle, Belle, Belle," my mother yells from her bed. I take this memory of mine and carve, the shavings curl and fall like the skin of an apple. She is an acute shape to me. I focus harder and harder until I get her pared down to an extreme miniature, to the density of a stone skidding on water. I slip this little stone shape, my mother, into my pocket where I can't hear it moan.

Around me the ocean expands like a dilating pupil. The longer and deeper the wake the clearer my future. Standing at the boat's bow, I am impervious to the wind or the wet or the cold. I am kept warm by the notion of my mother cut down to slivers. She'll surely wonder where I am, where her piece of pie went to, when I don't come home. Not to mention the receipt for the flowers.

In the cabinets of my island bungalow I store Gauloises, champagne, lost keys. I watercolor the wooden panels with scenes from my plays. The dining room table is long and empty and spread with linen. Outside the open window I see planes that I am piloting land and take off in rapid succession.

I step outside with skater's feet, my blades making snake bites in the sand. The honeysuckle on summer porches looks crisp and concise, chokecherry and wild rose bushes crouch low as I pass. It is a true road, true and positive and knowing. Heat fills my shoulders like warm blood and I breathe the blue of the sky and the pink of the strawflowers. The green grass is in my arms and legs and chest. My neck stretched out, my chin lifted, I am the daughter of a proud father.

Out of the crowd, a figure, luminous and white. I press my nails into the stale wood of the pier, I lean forward. The sky is breaking up around me, rumbling. It will be a thunderstorm, the night is coming down in thick strokes. Her outline is distinct to me, even as the boat pulls away slowly, as I stay on the pier.

Lost in the Last Act of *La Traviata*

> "Unforeseen joy never enters a sad heart
> without disturbing it."
> —Violetta, in Verdi's *La Traviata*

A t ten minutes to eight, I held a letter in front of the mailbox at Lincoln Center. *La Traviata* was about to begin, and in my wallet waited the ticket I had bought for nineteen dollars— because that was how cheap it could get, and because the man behind the counter wasn't cruel when I asked for the inexpensive seat.

That morning I had dressed up and even dug out my fur-collared coat. All day the collar had made gentle women my enemies. It was thirty-seven degrees, according to the clock in Times Square. I could see this and the time—7:51, 7:52—as other fur coats brushed by like buffalo. I wished some muse would lean out of a car window and say, "Go ahead! Take a risk!" But no angel came to help. Instead, I was nearly run over by the rich. "Slow down," an elderly man indicated to a cab with a whisk of his hand. Perturbed by the commotion, soon he would be swathed in opera.

I could have stood at the mailbox all night. I put the letter away and walked to the corner and back again, as if taking a running start would help.

✲

The man I loved cooed sweetly into his bedroom phone while I ate Saltines in his kitchen. We had spent a certain amount of time together, not more than I could review fully, given a half-hour, in cinematic, scene-by-scene splendor. Vincent spoke two languages: the quiet murmurings, the one-word answers required to get through an evening with me, and the brusque bullying voice he used with the boys, who called him Vince, as in, "Hey Vince, got any beer?" The longest sentence he ever used with me was, "I can't give you what you want." Undaunted, I had fashioned him into a lion or at very least a lion tamer.

As a little girl, I snuck through forests as the Lost Duchess Isabella. The Lost Duchess wore a brown cape and a long pointy hat with a little scarf at the end of it. The scarf bobbed insouciantly as the Lost Duchess waited at international ports for pirate-princes to return from jungle islands with small black velvet bags filled with diamonds. She was not materialistic so much as concerned with justice: the gems had been stolen from her frail sister by an evil emperor.

Evil was a word that thrilled the Lost Duchess. It was an unnamed but palpable evil that kept her running through the forest, at times delicately turning her pointy-hatted head, clasping the rough bark of an oak tree, to see if it had caught up to her yet. She owned a complete wardrobe somewhere, but for now she had only the clothes on her back—the Lost Duchess was on the lam. She had survived a shipwreck. She had swum miles in treacherous, shark-choked waters. Always looking back, always running forward, the Lost Duchess nonetheless had an impressive signature, and one day, when good conquered evil, when justice prevailed, she would sit home and knit socks by the fireplace and write out her adventures.

᛭

"You can type seventy-nine words per minute," a woman behind the desk at the first of five temporary agencies I went to that day had brightly revealed. I curled the rabbit collar of my coat underneath the cashmere, thrilled at my score. Lately, my dreams of happiness with Vincent—homesteading in Wyoming, pastry eating in New Orleans—had been joined by a determination to spend every spare second doing something productive. That's why I bought a ticket to the opera: it was my responsibility to witness, at least once, a performance of those strange sounds. And that, in addition to looming debt, motivated my search for a second job to supplement my income from the bookstore.

In the *For Office Use Only* part of the application, there was a place for this woman reviewing my skills to rate from one to five my poise, attire, articulation and appropriateness. What is appropriate here? I wondered. I was still cowed from my inability to answer question ten on page four: *Circle the word closest in meaning to "affect": handbag, change or strength.* I nodded energetically when the permanently placed office worker asked:

"Can you use Microsoft Word, WordPerfect, Wang, Macintosh? Will you work weekends? Will you accept receptionist work? Will you work anywhere?"

When I put my coat over the railing, an usher in a gold-trimmed circus vendor suit swooped down to tell me that nothing was allowed there. I pulled away the offending article and stuffed it behind my back where it remained during the show like a demanding pet. I was in the Family Circle, so high up I became dizzy. I looked over the railing. Who was in the front row? Was there anyone mimicking even more accurately than the French couple on my left (alternately whispering short phrases of adoration to one another and nipping a chocolate bar) proper opera etiquette?

The unsent letter poked out of my purse. As the lights went

down and the curtain went up, its whiteness gleamed like a flash-light. I was thinking about résumé format. Maybe I should list my accomplishments with bullets:

- Published poem in high school literary magazine.
- Spent three weeks on softball team one summer.
- Found coffee shop in New York with $2.00 breakfast special that includes bacon and juice.

In the first act of *La Traviata*, the virtuous whore Violetta responds favorably to the love of a nonpaying suitor, Alfredo. She has thus far been alone in life, though her bed has been crowded with johns—Sir John, Marquis John, Count John. She is fragile among the singing drinkers at the party in her parlor. From my perch up two hundred red-carpeted stairs, I couldn't see her face at all. I imagined she looked like the Lost Duchess. She was small and thin, with black hair, white skin, cheeks flushed with fever. Yet she could slam down champagne and these sounds came out of her like wild birds. No, no, no, Violetta wails, and there is a yes to her song, too, in the hums and valleys of the sounds. I had been running a finger up and down the jagged edge of my thumbnail, but by the end of the act, when lit chandeliers descended on web swings like giant glass spiders, my hands were still and lap-bound.

I had, in the spaces between Vincent's calls, become an ex-fiction writer. The story that finally stopped me was called "A Cold Place" and every time I tried to write it my fingers froze. It was the only story for me, it wasn't commercial at all, and besides that I couldn't write it anyway. I had become overwhelmed with rejection letters. I could no longer reconcile the assurances "the proof is in the pudding" with "all good things come to those who wait." I put my old and unpublished stories in a box labeled "The Early Years" and stuck it in my closet.

✳

For lunch that afternoon I sat on a bench and ate a plain bagel and drank a diet soda. I liked spending two dollars or less on lunch. I could justify spending that much. I had been to two employment agencies and had three more to go. My last appointment was at 5:30. I chewed the bagel slowly—it was a bit dry—and wrote Vincent a letter about how lionlike he was and about how I liked lions. As I wrote, I felt willful and excited: expressing myself made me breathless.

Violetta and Alfredo are living together in the second act. She is supporting them both by selling off some of her legs-spread acquisitions; he doesn't know of this for some feebleminded reason. Alfredo Senior, Germont I mean, demands of Violetta that she leave his son, the first man she has ever loved. Why does Violetta obey him? Like the Lost Duchess, Violetta is willing to sacrifice. But when Violetta goes from whore to slut and then to martyr, Alfredo, not knowing her secret virtue, condemns her.

While the two lovers on stage were together, the French *fille* next to me removed her hand from her beau's and took to sniffling into a hankie.

Violetta coughs at times, her cough innocuous as the next bend in the street.

At intermission, I took the letter out of my purse and used it to save my place. Love letters can be so useful. There were long lines for brownies and plastic cups of red wine; I bought a cup and leaned over the balcony. What if I spilled wine on a man below me? Would he notice? When I spoke to Vincent, for instance when I said, "I get very upset to think of you with other women," or "I like you so much, you mean so much to me," he nodded and said, "Yup." I thought he really did understand. Still, sometimes I considered saying something off-base, something I didn't mean, like "I enjoy seeing other men, too," to see what would happen.

⚜

At my fifth and final appointment for the day, a young man with no socks sat next to me in the waiting room. Magazines in employment agencies can be worse than in dentist offices: *Corporate Regulation and Its Assets, Statistical Analysis of Remote Objects, 1991 Financial Review of Similar Sounding Subsets.* I looked for one with pictures, but the sockless man had the only copy of *People.* To fill out the application, I was given a pink pen with an oval plastic attachment to keep it from sliding off desks. It was here that I couldn't help but lie a little on the paperwork. The interviewers had all smiled so greedily when I said I had ten years of computer experience, but said nothing when I told them I could recite the first book of the *Odyssey* from memory. I smiled when they smiled, as you do when you hear a joke in a foreign language. I smiled like an idiot. Why not give this one something to really sink her teeth into? Hence:

Employment History: Governess, 1876-1879; Rodeo Rider, 1904-1908; Charles Manson Devotee, 1970.

The Lost Duchess was independently wealthy; she didn't have to think about the pros and cons of working as a secretary versus public relations assistant. She could spend all her time battling evil in her own escapist fashion. She wasn't like Superman, she couldn't catch criminals or fly off rooftops. If she got the little baggie of diamonds for her poor discarded sister, that would be enough. She could go back to the castle and write her memoirs in fancy script.

The $4.75 glass of wine made me feel even dizzier, plus I experimented with taking my distance glasses off and putting them on again while I waited for the third and last act, not really knowing if what I wanted to look at was near or far. Standing in line for the wine, I wondered if anyone there besides me had been looking for a job as a word processor that day. After that last interview—the woman reading my application didn't even blink when she read my employment history (perhaps she was tired, or just used to immortal Manson-followers applying for jobs there at Elite Personnel where "Excellence Is the Watchword")—I had an hour to kill before going to Lincoln Center. I spent it sketching an intricate design on the envelope's border.

Whores do it for money and sluts do it for pleasure; I fit in the second category. Maybe there is something that binds these women anyway—the will to hold your hands in a fire or cross a street without looking both ways. Bad feeling invades a slut's body like a creepy-crawler, a stain, if she loves her partner. Getting money for sex always seemed uglier to me in its calculation than any mistake made in the rainstorm heart: the unrehearsed, slutty gestures.

I respected a man who could keep his dick in his pants when confronting temptation on the street corner or party corner—though not much, I mean, I didn't think this feat deserved an award. Yet I also wanted a man who knew the pleasure of absolute disorder. To keep Vincent to myself, I had determined, I would have to shoot every woman in the world.

As Violetta sang her songs in the short, short last act of *La Traviata*, I felt like the one with a fever. She looked as little as a beetle in her white nightgown in the white blankets on a divan spotlighted stage center. Love letter filed away, I felt nervous. Lipstick reapplied, I wondered where the French kissers were. They had not returned to their seats after intermission. I missed them now. I wanted them to live happily ever after.

Violetta was sick with consumption, but maybe she'd get better. Her maid attended to her. The words she sang were brief red birds, cardinals on their way to brighter worlds. I pulled my coat around my shoulders and gripped the fur collar.

⚹

I've tried to arrange you by element, I had written, and edited later into *I am a hopeless organizer. I didn't know love before* was a line that still worried me. I wanted to rip the envelope open and cross it out. I wanted to replace the word *love* with *slight attraction.* My wan stories and trailing poems had probably bent to the same rule as all my previous letters: Only write things that leave you disinterested and limp. Don't excite the reader.

Who's at the door? It is Alfredo—come at last to apologize for being a loser. The splatter of sound coming from the orchestra was what I heard as the Lost Duchess, running through the forest, pointy hat on, mission determined. Only a Lost Duchess feels the pull of her kingdom, the warmth of the fire in the grand ancestral hall. Only a Lost Duchess feels the glimmer of a candle handed to her as she ascends the castle stairs into the bed chamber. Only in cold, sharky waters can said Lost Duchess imagine, most accurately, the deep warmth of his hands on her shoulders. I never wanted to make metaphor. What is the perfect unkindness? It is the perfect opera.

Violetta shrieks with what seems like pleasure, but it is her last breath ever. She flings herself back into the soft downy pillows in a parody of herself and is gone from this world.

The curtain fell and the audience moved into applause. Violetta had died, and she had felt love—what could be better? But then the curtain rose again and the dead woman, the one wrecked from love, opened her eyes and leaned forward. She was sitting, smiling, rising from her deathbed. She rose like a drowsy child, the awakened one. Her white gown trailed behind her as she walked forward, boldly, strongly now, and took the hands of the two male leads. Violetta was alive! She smiled and curtsied to the audience, catching one of the bouquets flying in her direction like a softball. The opera was over; now she would go out to dinner.

When I got outside, it was raining heavily. I had no umbrella. I pulled the bunny thing up around my neck and hurried, head down, toward the subway. *La Traviata* had been the epitome of my heart, it was the sly twinship of love and pain, merged forever. I saw the mailbox through the storm, in front of the slur of cabs and stampeding affluence. In the wake of the dark tubercular drama, it was easy to open the little blue door and let the letter drop into the dark air. Even my small love story, the short libretto of my relationship with Vincent, seemed insignificant.

Twin

My brother loved words and he loved to build things.

One summer afternoon I sat on the porch studying my toes while he constructed something out of wood. He was stretching one of Mother's lace pillowcases into a sharp triangle, nailed to a broomstick and a plywood box. He breathed noisily. I was annoyed. I tried to engage him in one of our games.

"Whale, wary, washbasin," I said.

West didn't reply. He had picked up a saw; the boat had an unevenness in the stern.

"Wilderness, worry, window."

The saw got stuck in the wood and when West tried to shake it loose it sounded like thunder.

"Words, women, wood," I suggested. "West?"

But my brother had fallen into a steady silence. He had a gone look I hadn't seen in him before.

I grabbed the saw and pulled it out in a frenzy. The saw held over my head, I jumped up and down on the moist, peeling porch and shrieked:

"Wind! Whip! Worship!"

West looked at me. He turned away and walked toward the garage. I kept jumping and yelling until he was behind the house, thinking he'd look back and see me and laugh with me. But he

95

didn't. I sat down, letting the saw drop. Black ants approached my feet. I took a bobby pin out of my hair and lanced one. The two sides kept moving even after they were apart.

He had big blue eyes, the size of lesser men's hearts.

One August night I lay on my bed around eleven o'clock. It had been hot all day and my window was wide open. I lay on top of my sheets in a loose white nightgown with long satin ribbons and shoulder straps. I was rewriting names in a new address book. Some people I left out this time, I used pencil for the rest. I heard The Knock, and of course he knew to come in.

We were older then, but things weren't so different. We went out into the world and came back, ready to listen. We moved and spoke by instinct. The differences we did have were soft spots that only we knew. With crescent-shaped claws we dug in, never letting go.

West sat on the bed. I leaned my knees toward the wall and held my hand out to him. He took it, and each of our fingers came together until the vulnerable webbing touched and our thumbs lay, his above mine, as one. I looked into my reflection. His eyes were deep enough to dive into, and swim. History stopped with our gaze. Words were useless.

"I'm leaving, Riva. I'm joining the navy. I'm going to war."

Something in my eyes made him stop. Who knows what he saw there, but it wasn't a woman waving a kerchief on the pier; I wasn't the kind of woman to welcome a brother back home. And for the first time in my life, I saw his eyes darken into great pools of deceit. My pillow and bed and bedroom began to crumble. I sat on top of a sand mountain. The turn of an hour.

I cut my hair to the crown and put on his clothes and shoes and cologne. I saluted him in the living room. He frowned, looked out the window, and then looked back at me.

"You had better keep your head."

96

I remembered the night I went out on a date, my first. West was outside, ripping great pricker bushes out of the stone wall surrounding the house.

"Good-bye, West," I said, fidgeting.

He didn't answer. The horn sounded again.

"West?"

My brother pulled the vine with all his might. The wall burst as from the force of water and rocks tumbled down. West sat on his hands. He had that distant look again.

"Riva?" he began.

I walked toward the car.

We wanted to take the rowboat out one last time before he left.

I stood on the rock couched in black mud and skunk cabbage and leaned on an old tree. West, already launched, held out his hand. His shirtsleeves were rolled up over his brown arms. He squinted, waiting for me to take his hand and get in. His look reflected all of my misgivings and none of them. I had to trust him.

My foot slipped as I reached. The olive canal rose up and my arms clawed at his legs, the seat, anything—my legs were dragging in the thick water behind me. Our faithful *Magnificence* began drifting away with me half-in and half-out. Finally West pulled me all the way in, and I sat crumpled and wet in the boat's belly. The rocking stopped. I swept back my hair and looked at my brother gravely. We laughed until tears were in our eyes.

"You can't go," I said, different tears coming.

West kneeled down and put his arms around me. I felt his sculptured cheek on mine. His breath was all I could breathe.

"If I don't go, I won't be myself."

I knew that.

"Let's row," he said, after a while.

We picked up the oars and rowed the way we used to, one oar each, impractical but satisfying.

"If they send you to the front will you go?"

✻

He loved to build things. We woke up immediately in those days, like cats. We lived on instincts, I've said.

A letter from the president. A country I'd never heard of. A check.

My toes are like pebbles, smoothed by nighttime waves. My hair reaches, drifts, untangles.

What I remember now are the word games. War, woe, willow. Water, whisper, West. The words add up to nothing some days, so I stand by the ocean, and let the sounds come to me, one by one, overlapping. The sun and the sand and the water fill me, and then they run out again. Through the hole where once was a brother, where room for a brother waits. So I try to patch it up with words, with remembering, a semblance of what things were. But he doesn't answer. Though I gain something, too, on those days. The ocean. A silvery indication of more.

Henry's Suitcase

He stares at the sidewalk: it has a beauty to it. He walks at half-pace to the young, the new bloodlines. The sun is his friend, anyway. The sun has stuck around.

He will get plain yogurt and rye crackers, this time without seeds, at the grocery. Not the one where the clerk taps her foot at him and picks her nails while he counts the change in his palm, but the other store, with the softball-coach manager, whose muscles jump and extend. But the sidewalk goes on forever. Didn't he just pass this hydrant? What day is today?

Henry, on the other hand, walked quickly, skipping practically. He hurried to catch up with Henry, to hear what he had to say. He wondered how Henry's world related to the one of errands and dentistry. It seemed to take it away.

The newspaper lies on the kitchen table. Each copy has the same obituary. Everyone walks slow these days. He eyes the newspaper from a distance, drinking a concoction meant to simulate coffee. Henry didn't read the paper. He used it for a hat, a blanket, a toy boat, wrapping paper—but he was the news of the day.

He pulls the suitcase out from under his bed. He runs his hand over the tattered edges. It's funny how things can get old. He touches two pairs of pants, three starched white shirts, three pairs of boxer shorts, a cardigan, a tie, a jacket. He opens the shaving bag and fingers the razor, the shaving cream, the soap, the wash-cloth. In the front pocket, behind a leather pouch containing tie clips, cuff links and a shoehorn, are two one-way tickets for a steamship abroad.

He writes:

It's an obscure fault to drop dead to the ground. But you live on, in ecstasy. I am the cipher here. People turn away in the street, they are embarrassed when they see my sagging eye sockets, they cut me down. You still drink from a wine glass, big gulpfuls, the liquid shining on your lips. You sing while I pray. You shout while I stumble to the laundry, while I watch myself deteriorate, while the life in me rots away.

You told me that life was a club. That, sitting in a restaurant, we are really in a fraternity of the living. The club is exclusive, you said, with infights going on down its wide avenues, its sunny paths divided by thickets. Children run their hot, red-stained hands over the bushes, and men and women stay cool inside, lay-ing down cards. The days repeat themselves, and it is sweet and expected, how at five o'clock the sun withdraws in long lazy stretches over the tabletops, the empty chairs, the half-drawn cur-tains. Everyone is full of minor complaints, but they have mem-bership cards tucked in their back pockets. They wake up in the morning, dress in clothes that carry their own scents, drink cups of chocolate. The club is ghastly in its turnover, there is no repeat membership. The decisions are made by grand cabinet, seated from left to right: a pine cone, two beetles, a fragrance, a brick, and the presiding chairman, a slug.

You lied.

He rips the page from the notebook and places it in the frying pan. There, with worm-eaten fingers, he lights the paper with a wooden match, and the low flame sweeps over the page, greedy for it, falling down exhausted at the end of a thrilling affair.

He will buy toilet paper, peanuts, distilled water. When he cork-screws his body to look at the woman passing on his left, she looks at him bright and square, smiles radiantly and tries to hand him a quarter. "Bitch! Shit!" he sputters. Henry had the women choking on their salads.

"The milk is gone," he claims, at the grocery store. A couple dressed in leather passes by.

The light hums. He looks up. The ceiling is falling down. He stares at the bacon, cottage cheese, pickles, ham. Another shopper, unwieldy with a basket, jostles him.

"The milk is gone. The ceiling is falling down."

The shopper apologizes.

He looks at his hands: the trembling has begun. He holds one hand in another, trying to calm down. Perhaps the milk has been moved, he reasons. He walks down the aisle. But no, it's gone. He strokes his hand. It's not his hand that trembles, it's the building. The building is shaking, the ceiling is falling down, the milk is gone.

"The milk is gone. The building is shaking. The ceiling is falling down," he says, looking around. Where is his friend? He needs someone. "Where is my friend?" he calls out. "My friend is gone!"

He turns the radio on. Static is coming through the lines. If only he could get a clear station. He can't get a clear station, he needs a clear sound.

Then it comes. An orchestra. He used to close his eyes and try to separate out the instruments. Now it's the other way around: the sounds have pulled away from each other like icebergs on a warming polar ocean, where cold means life, and warmth is a dark land. He shuts the radio off again. Sitting by the half-open window, he looks out at the street. Henry. Henry is gone.

�֍

He writes:

There is a kind of worm that smooths a path for himself underground. As the rings around his body bulge and squeeze, he makes a sweet sound. When he stops moving, the song ends. All of mankind wants to find one. But we haven't been able to capture him. He disappears as the scientist comes trudging out in the field, kicking his steel spade into the ground. He stops moving, he quiets down, he is gone. The scientist yawns and goes home. The worm stretches again, curves toward a schoolyard, in song.

You told me about life. But things are different now. People don't know how to behave. Noodles come in three colors and soap has vitamins. I wish we could talk. You scared me, but you calmed me down.

He blows the black feathers into the trash can.

In the morning the phone rings. It will be bad news. His stomach turns. Even a light breakfast can't be eaten most days, unless, by some fluke, all his components are in order. He certainly can't receive phone calls before the lunch hour.

"Hello, Dad? It's Dora. How are you feeling?"

"Fine. Pretty good."

"The kids are asking about you. You don't visit us anymore."

"Well."

"Listen, I know you're probably busy, I won't keep you. But we need to talk about this real estate matter."

"I don't feel well. I think I have a stomach upset."

"What if the lawyer comes to your apartment?"

"No! It's not clean."

"You'll go to his office, then? How about Monday? Is Monday all right?"

"OK, OK. Can you hold on?"

"Of course."

He hurries to the bathroom. In a couple of minutes, when he returns, his daughter is no longer on the phone.

He gathers up his umbrella, jacket, galoshes. He has a list. But the keys? Not by the newspaper. Not on the hook, or on the windowsill, unless they fell into the street (he peers down). He sits by the table, his jacket and galoshes on, rubber folding awkwardly into his skin. He'll just wait here until they return.

The phone rings again: "Hi, Dad." Seems there's a rush to those papers. He must go to the bank and to his safe-deposit box. Would he do it now? She'll be over in an hour. "I've lost my keys," he says. "Well then," she responds, "I'll come now."

He walks to the bank with his daughter. He walks on the beach with Henry. When they arrive the security guard is turning the lock into place, smiling out at him from behind the glass. He stabs at his social security card with a hard yellow finger.

"If you could only keep your wits about you."

The daughter smells strongly of perfume. She is walking around the room picking things up—the newspaper, his orange peels, his frying pan—and putting them in disorder. As she wipes out the frying pan with detergent and water, she explains things, turning her head toward him. He sits by the window in a state of panic. Drying her hands, she comes over and gives him a kiss on the head. "Too cold, Daddy?" She pulls the window down.

Henry held out his hand from the rowboat's middle. "C'mon, then, buddy," he said.

The chilly water lapped up around his sneakers. He felt it on his toes. He was in the mud with the snails and seaweed, and the tide was coming in faster, the waves were getting strong. It was a delirious, jumping-off-a-building sensation; he leaned forward, grit and salt water on his teeth and tongue, and then he lunged.

He writes. He burns. The mail comes. A statement from the hospital, he owes them a thousand dollars. A notice from the health insurance company, his policy is about to run out. A clipping from his daughter, his old neighbor gave up the ghost. A letter forwarded from the post office, stamped "Lost."

Lost. Henry's handwriting shakes in his hand. The postmark, the date of the would-be journey. The letter, communication with the dead and gone.

"Who is this man you keep mumbling about? Just another figment of your imagination, like the draft in the apartment, or your stomach problems. You really should take care of yourself, Dad, stay under the covers."

It is, in fact, an explanation. It has to be that. The letter is on the shelf, unopened. He holds his stomach and moans. Everything comes to this, then, funneling down to the shape of the words in an envelope, one explanation, one tomb. He holds onto the raft as the tide comes.

The pills wear off in the middle of the night. He opens his eyes, and the rocking has quieted, the storm has gone down. He stares at the ceiling, gray as the sky moments before dawn. The glimmer in the corner of his eyes should have been stars. In the darkness he feels young.

Getting up and sitting on the side of his bed—light hiding behind the curtains, sifting in the front door—he drags his fingers through his hair, thick as a broom. His shoulders loom in the shadows with gentle strength, treelike repose.

He takes the letter in one hand and carries it to the kitchen. He stands at the stove. The white gleaming porcelain reminds him of a fishing song he knows, about the prison in every belly, the green sea over every cast of white bones. The black burners on the stove swim up at him like giant heads in a reverse ocean. They want air. He flips on the flame.

Lit in blue, his face is strange as a flower. His mouth, ripe and blooming, looks as if it might say something. But there is no sound, except for one letter, as it burns.

Charisma

The most important thing I can say about myself is that I knew how to sew aprons with clarity and thoroughness. The aprons I sewed were blue with red rickrack around the edges, they had big puffy pockets, they tied in bows in the back. I sewed them by hand. I'd been sewing them since I was a child. My parents showed me the craft.

The second most important thing about me was that I believed I was not alone in the world. I believed that somewhere, I had a perfect match.

He was not human, I am convinced. How could he have been? He was the thorny stem of a rosebush. He moved his hand like that, and then there was the petal and the submersion in softness. I remember what he smelled like. He didn't tell me his name, but he gave me that smell like a diamond ring couched in black.

It was so easy for him. He turned to me and brushed something off my shoulder, and I felt immeasurably lighter.

He said: "You deserve better."

"Better than what?"

"You can make better aprons than that, you can make ball gowns. You don't need red rickrack. I see that you can make white satin dresses. Is that right? Am I right?"

"You are right," I whispered, and kept whispering, into my drink, into the night. I saw white dresses dancing in the sky, beautiful sleeves and long trains and buttons up the back.

"Tell me about the dresses you can make."

I can't describe the way he smelled, and I can't describe my childhood, which went on and on like a faulty script. I grew up in this small town, and I was ordinary in every way. Except sometimes when I scratched mosquito bites behind my legs, I folded my body into a cricket shape. In those moments I was as tuneful as a violin.

I'd like to explain something. It wasn't that I thought my perfect match would necessarily come to me, that he necessarily lived on earth at that time in history. It was a possibility, though. He could have lived. He could have understood the cricket shape in my arms and legs at night, when I was alone, and my aprons were folded in the drawer next to me.

What did he want from me? I could make all his family (Could he have a family? Could he have origins?) blue aprons with red rickrack. I turned to the man whose name I didn't know with a new smile on my face, a white dress smile, a luminescence.

When I turned to him, when in my hands I held out the raw material, the uncut fabric, he knew—didn't he?—what it meant. He didn't ask for it. I gave it to him because my soul got caught on a breeze in the dark windowless night, and it leapt out of its hiding place and skittered off, twirling and skidding by the man's feet.

I was slightly breathless without my soul. I was a shape to dress in an apron or a white dress. I thought: he will dress me in the gown. I had discarded the apron and I was naked—less than naked, I was empty space. I stood there, as space can stand, and looked at him without a name.

I used to assume the cricket position in bed and close my eyes, being an immensity of aloneness. This had limited appeal. I let the pitter-patter of the waves of my knowledge of the perfect match lull me to sleep.

Garbage and souls flitted in the night. I no longer had a career. I could no longer make aprons. He had known it. He knew I could no longer, could never again, sew a row of red rickrack on the edge of a pretty apron. Never, never again would this be good enough. I would sew reams and reams of white satin. I would stitch two hundred pearl buttons. I would embroider.

But one must have a customer. One must sell the dress. I had the list of apron-wearers. I walked the neighborhood on Saturdays with my suitcase of folded blue fabric. I peddled. I let the humble women make deposits, use layaway, pay with checks. But what of the white dress?

His eye had a diamond in it. And when he turned away from me on the balcony there, when I had seen my soul skitter out into the streets, when I had lost my career, I could no longer see this. I was an empty space, without any clothes on. I walked—the way empty spaces walk—around him, around his side, over to the front of his rosebush body, and I again set my soulless eyes on him.

A smell invades your nostrils. It moves into your body and rec-reates there. I knew the thorn and the soft petal in his glance, I had sniffed around him like that.

"What is your name?" I asked.

I walked home without a dress, without a soul, without a prom-ise.

The cricket shape of my body needs no explanation, and there is the outline of this sharpness even without my soul, like the lines that connect the stars in a constellation chart.

I would no longer be happy making aprons. Is this a step in the right direction? The day would come, and spread over the black night of diamonds like a white satin gown.

Legend

D ebbie woke to a big black form hanging over her head. She turned on the small lamp with the pom-pom shade, sat up in her nightie and squinted at her mother. The woman, dressed in sequins and a boa, asked: "May I have a little seat?"

Debbie made room for her on the bed. Her mother's presence, thick with perfume and cigarette smoke, shrunk her room down to dollhouse proportion.

"I know your birthday's coming, and of course we're getting you the pony as we've already discussed. But this is something I wanted to give you in addition. You wear it on your breast. My mother gave it to me, now I'm giving it to you. You will like it."

In her large almond hands the self-made woman cradled something like a baby bird. It was a brooch, a circle pin clustered with diamonds and pearls. Debbie saw the pin moving toward her chest and the thin fabric over her skin. Her mother's hands moved like trucks toward their destination. In her exhilaration—getting rid of the piece of jewelry, was it, or the joy of giving?—she tore the white cotton and pricked her daughter's flesh.

I always made sure they were dead before I did anything. I held the bird's head under the water in the toilet bowl, rolled the mouse's eyes up moony and wide. I wanted to know: where does pain come from? Is it in the blood or the bone?

At the card shop where I work I like the way the cards are organized, it gives life more of a shape. There is friendship, marriage, death, birthday from uncle, condolences to son. There is sickness, birth, and going away. There is *I'm sorry,* and there is *It's your mistake.*

My mother left home when I was twelve, old enough to be a boarder at school. She left me in the care of my father. I've tried to lead a simple life. I thought if I could do that I'd be all right. But I have these dreams where my skin is the consistency of gelatin, or all the lamps in the house are powered by animal blood. The dreams keep coming. I tried church. I opened the hollow door and stood in the back. The priest was so far away, he was on the other end of a long red carpet. He spoke in valiant terms about courage. On my way home I tapped my fist on the fence until my knuckles bled. In the space between pickets I realized that I would not be happy until I got her back.

Two men wait in the periphery, while Debbie's mother talks to the luminary of the moment. The chosen one smiles with her, nods with her, breathes in her cigarette smoke. Her mink stole is half-gone over her shoulder. A hat the color of copper tilts over her peacock eyes, her lips form an Egyptian smile.

"The ocean itself is overrated, *I* know that. It's just a big puddle, a water-weary piece of earth. What's all the fuss? The ocean knows its own worth.

"It's not that I have any great gift, it's that other women are stunted. We've all got the same limbs, the same brain, the same opportunities. Have you looked at my nose? I mean, really looked at it. It's awful. Can't you see that? Some women would be incapacitated by this nose, most women would. It's repulsive, an unearthly schnauze, a nursery school Play-Doh attempt. But you probably didn't even notice it, did you? Hah. Figures. You're just like the rest.

"Look at her over there, the one with the feet. Notice how she moves. She moves like an apology. Do you see that? And how do you think she is in bed? A real animal? Yes, I bet. Sex appeal just exuding from that dry-toast hip jerk like a subterfuge. Almost exhausting, just *thinking* about sex with that girl. I mean, the aroma is overwhelming.

"People live as if this is one of many chances they'll have. They think they'll be reincarnated all over the place. It's a pathetic mystery, how people watch a television show on a Saturday night, sharing a worn-down couch with a worn-out mate, turn it off at twelve-thirty, and, while walking toward the bathroom to brush and floss their teeth, they think: *The beauty of that show is positively overwhelming. I am going to be like that woman someday.* Someday. And they go to sleep, maybe with a short hug of beastly ordinariness, and swallow that sedative Someday.

"No wonder people spend so many hours calculating ways to shit on the taxi driver, the waiter, the clerk.

"My family? Well, my father's great-great-grandfather came over on the *Mayflower*. Yes. He was a pilgrim. Not one of the famous ones. He was a servant. A pilgrim-servant. He wrote all about it in his diary. Did you know that the pilgrims were hot on sex slavery? Oh, not the publicized kind. They just did their s & m jingles in the privacy of their own one-room shacks. Can you imagine? Sex among the brooms and black woolen caps. A little eroticism on the straw mattress, hanging by ropes on a four-trunk bed. All the rosy-faced pilgrim kids turned their faces toward the diminishing fire, watched the drizzle come down the chimney stack.

"My mother was very ordinary. Very. Before she met my father and he stole her away to Key West, she lived in suburbia with her mom and dad. Well, they were her foster parents. Her other parents died when she was twelve. Mysteriously, yes. They didn't know if it was murder or what. Apparently it was a Toll House cookie baking accident. One of those Saturday afternoons parents are always so fond of. You know, gather around kiddies, let's do some baking. Here's a little project, and *you* can help. I guess the oven blew. Their heads were smooshy like two big melted chocolate chips. Young Cindy was in the study when the firemen came, playing with her Beth doll. Beth, from *Little Women*? She was the sweet one. My mom's favorite. She wore a pink pinafore, a white blouse with puffy sleeves, and her brunette hair always curled up. *Naturally* Mom was in shock. Of course.

"Yes, two. I was the youngest.

"Thank you. The doctors say I had better stop or I'll get skin cancer. But *what* do doctors know about life? What do they know? I've been tan as a nut since I was a little girl. I grew up on the sand. I spent whole afternoons chewing salt-crusted hair and drinking lemonade. Never bought my own lemonade in my life. Let's get out of this dreary place, I've really got to go.

"Of course I'm lonely when I'm alone. What kind of question is that? When I'm alone, I don't know who I am. I become a watchamajig."

The bus seat is worn at the edges, as if I'm not the first to make this journey. It's midnight, and I don't know where I'm going. Finding her isn't going to be easy. But I suspect I know where to begin looking. At the most fashionable openings. At the president's ball.

Fried-egg sandwiches with Rob. Sex in places where I can't wash the diaphragm jelly off my fingers and it dries into scales on my skin. It's smelly. It's a mess on my hands and in between my legs. But who's complaining? Rob is. He says I should go on the pill. But if I ever have a child, a baby girl, I want her to have every chance for living, every single chance alive.

My body crawls with grime and sweat but I close my eyes and pretend I'm in bed, my head on a pillow, wrapped up to the neck in clean white sheets. Even under duress she kept up appearances, her eyes beating the air in strong defiant sweeps, her tongue lashing those around her with sweet caresses. I expect she's the same now as she was then. Her wrists bleeding and her shanks pale and trembling with disappearance, she'd still twitch her nose if she saw me, and motion for a cigarette.

"Darling, you've always been my favorite in the whole wide world. Now be a dear and get those matches on the sink there."

"But Mother, you're bleeding. What have you done?"

"Don't worry, french fry. I'm just bloodletting. Just a little old-fashioned bloodletting for the holidays. I'll come out stronger in the end. I'm getting fatigued now. Please take the phone off the hook. Be a good girl and get me my purse. We need a quart of milk. Run down and get my glasses. Be a dear. I know you always. Loved me. I expect you will begin brushing your hair properly? Take off the phone. Don't talk to anyone. Leave. Me."

Rob says he loves me but I don't know what that means. It makes me feel foggy. He must love me, to come with me across country. He says that when he gets out of ROTC he's going to be a fighter-jet pilot and blow the commies away. He's very patriotic like that. I don't understand those things so I don't know what to say. He always looks big and strong. I just watch his fists pound the bus seat. Then later he'll put his arm around my waist, or pinch my thigh, and say: "When're we going to get married?"

The sign says welcome to a new state.

"You are quite a lover, darling. I haven't felt so close to the stars since . . .

"Pass me a cigarette, baby. You *are* the naughty one.

"Oh, I'm not thinking about anything. Dreaming? How could I be dreaming if I am where I would be if I dreamed of being somewhere? I'm right where I want to be. Some tropical island, sure, that's the standard fantasy. But I don't believe in fantasy, I believe in living. One tiny fantasy comes into your world and you know you've failed. I like to live right now, right here. And if I don't like what I'm doing, I change it. No problem. No worry. You're being silent now. Do you have a little fantasy? Have I inadvertently stepped on my little pussycat's toes? My pussywhipped sweetie?

"I can't abide people who are lower than me. They remind me of the thick dregs in a bottle of cabernet. I only drink the pure jewel drink, the liquid sheen."

Debbie is a drunk at a Christmas party. The family, all dressed in velvet, dozes to a piano sonata by a young nephew. She, the drunk, stumbles in with a transistor radio. Full blast, the news story breaks over the holiday scene, like a bomb of the smelly, nonromantic variety. *Underneath the Oriental rug the house is burning,* she claims. All the guests look toward their feet doubtfully. She goes on: *Soon your eyeballs will pop out and your genitals will hang loose from their perch like melted cheddar.* The others look at each other, haughty and sure. Their laughter reaches her ears like a monotonous rain, a slow priestly rain that knows no end.

The woman licks her lips. Twice. As she watches the movie, the pre-release screening. Her face beats tan and gray with the passing of light on the screen. Her lips are dry and withered. She has taken many drugs at different times in her life to counteract aging in the various parts of her body, to loop together the fractures in her mind. She doses her skin with medications, Retin-A, exfoliant, bronzing gel. But nothing, no Chanel lipstick, takes away the parched feeling around her lips and mouth, the famine that leaves her face exposed.

I'm always careful, but I'm always unsure. That's where Rob helps me. He takes things into his own hands. He can make all those big decisions in life: what to spend money on, where to go when the movie is over. I have made just this one decision. But today, Rob said he wants to go home. When he told me that I felt black behind the eyeballs. I felt like pulling my teeth out and throwing them on the floor. "But we're only in Virginia," I said. "Don't you want to see the U.S.S. *Intrepid*?"

I tried to go to him, hug him, make him feel better. But he got awfully testy. His big patriotic arms pushed me to the floor. Then he felt contrite. We fucked in the motel hall, by the ice crusher. We're back on the bus now.

Once I didn't kill before the science project began. It was the neighbor's yapping dog, he had been hit by a car. He was nearly dead, I guess, but not quite. He was on the side of the road, looking peaceful and quiet, except he had this look in his eyes. He seemed to be concentrating very hard on living. I kneeled by him and his cow eyes stared at me, sidehinged in their sockets, as if he were waiting for me to do something. Didn't he know I hated him? He should have just looked away from me, ignored me there on the road and gone on dying. A dog's toe makes a good lucky charm, I thought, taking out my pocketknife.

When I got home, I went to bed right away. Mother always liked it when I slept.

Debbie inserts her diaphragm in the rocking lavatory of the bus. They are in Maryland. The blue stink of the toilet splashes up the sides of the steel rim. It is three in the morning and Rob woke her up. He is very insistent at times. She supposes that is what will make him so successful in the army: he goes that extra mile.

In the bus seat she had been dreaming. She was in a ballroom, dressed in a long blue dress. The sleeves were covered with baby pearls, and she clasped a sparkly clutch. A man she has never met (how did she get that face?) was looking at her from across the stage. She was telling her boarding school teachers she was a success. The man started yelling things at her. She couldn't hear what he said. She stood immobile in her buffed-satin shoes, unable to speak.

"Life is meant for laughter, if you can't laugh then you should cry. A good cry is also one of the pleasures of life. A solid heartbreak is good for the skin."

The spilled capsules were on the bathroom floor when she brushed her teeth before school. The bus seats flip forward one after another, each one revealing a new, terrifying face. Her hands are her mother's hands, they stick to her like kidskin. Rob will take care of her, he'll sit by her. He won't look at her face and ask what on earth is wrong.

"I'm not doing anything. Does a woman have to be doing something to sit up in her own bed at night. I'm just thinking, thinking . . .

"I'm thinking about the moon. The moon there, can you see it? Just this side of the curtain. That moon looks happy tonight, romantic. I'm not sentimental, but I am a bit of a historian. I'm remembering that same moon as I saw it once—when I was a teenager, a mere girl, and for the first time in my life someone stood me up. Oh, yes, it's happened to me. I lead a tragic life. It's surprising I can withhold all this love on my own, just one heart pumping blood and passion. Withhold? I mean withstand, silly pumpkin. I was waiting for him on the boardwalk at night. I could hear the lapping waves, they sounded ferocious, as if they were getting nearer, but I couldn't see them at all in the mist. It was late, very late, but finally, in the distance, I saw a shape, a man—I could just make out his face and hands. I ran over, I was so relieved. Until I got close. Then I saw it wasn't my date at all. 'Whoa, miss,' the man said. I remember his leer, and how he held my arm when I turned away. Perhaps I was an apparition for him, too. . . .

116

"The moon? Yes, the moon reminded me of that. Be a darling and pass the lighter."

Debbie has reached Port Authority. Rob is nowhere to be found. They got off the bus and he said he was leaving.

Debbie is leafing through the phone directory, one page after the other. She hears a rumbling over her shoulder. She has a funny feeling, as if she has a good shot at winning the raffle. Maybe not first, but second prize.

Tate J 362 E 63 404-9043

She's thinking of her old red diary. She's reading about herself, as if she just now found the miniature key. She sees words that she wrote, words that she's never seen before. Little things, but real: *I went to the grocer today. I saw my new flame in the hall.* She says the words to herself in the street.

Debbie's mother is in her apartment drying her nails when the bell rings. Who could it be? Flowers? The dry cleaning?

"Damn their timing," she says, swinging her legs off the sofa, nestling her feet into fur-puffed high heels.

"Hello?"

The doorman announces a Debbie.

There is a pause before she answers him.

"Debbie? I know of no such person. Tell her to leave."

The doorman conveys the message.

"Can I just leave her something, then?" Debbie asks, smiling sweetly. She takes a blue box out of her jean-jacket pocket. She opens it up and puts a furry, clawed something by the circle pin. She gives the box to the doorman.

"I'm a homespun woman, really. I spent my life just trying to get along, to be a good mother, a good wife. Yes, my daughter. She's off and running now. I expect she's having a good time without me. She was always so *needy,* you know? How boring."

✳

I believe in legend. If you try hard to make something happen, it will. This month, at the card shop, it's the unicorn. The unicorn, you know, was a mythical creature. He would lay his head on the lap of a beautiful princess and she'd sing him to sleep. I believe in unicorns. Rob, my fiancé, thinks I'm silly. So when he comes back from the war, I'll put all my stuffed animals away, back in the closet where they belong. What war? I don't know.

The Toreador

The history of an eclipse. I might go on a trip someday. Quit my job and go. The promises they make me won't keep me alive past July. Just quit, and go.

My red stockings sliced the path in front of me, sharp scissors in the snow. Grandmother stood behind the screen door. I concentrated on the monkeys tied to my laces until she reached for us, grabbing the thin air around my sister and me as if she were a sleepwalker, as if she were blind. She gave Carrie a kiss first and I knew mine was coming. I heard Dad's car go.

Mom was going to the grocery store to buy the usual things. My ballet class just over, I walked home in five o'clock shadow, early November, pointing my toes toward the water. I was a happy snail, and I sang. We all knew the way to McLellans. You took a left out of our driveway and followed Englebrook to the bottom of the hill. Left again on South Street, over the bridge, right at the intersection, and the grocery store was on your right, across from Carvel. If Carrie and I were with her sometimes we'd get a cone.

We had planned to see the Barnum and Bailey circus the next

weekend. She knew how I liked elephants, and she wouldn't have said it if it weren't true.

Summers I held Dad's hand and he left me off by the breakwater. Cold, early morning air brushed seashells into my hair. It was a town of late sleepers. Only the gulls and me, on the rocks, stretching our wings in the morning. One day I found a hard-pack of Winstons and a lighter on a smooth place on the stone. The cigarettes looked rich and delicious, but I left them alone. I flicked the lighter a couple of times and watched the blue flame turn into faces before I walked home.

At my office there is little color, and I am not one to mask that with mugs from home, framed photos or postcards. At the office it's not really gray, like sky gray or sweater gray or stone gray, it is unheard of, uncompromising gray: the gray of absence.

In Provincetown my colors were my own, the universe became me. Ten thousand countries rolled into one. Gazing past the ocean I did see Curaçao. I saw ships and shores beyond the immutable horizon. I had a pair of glasses, kaleidoscopes, and I could turn the horizon on its side, just by tilting. Rushing out, the waters, in my dream.

The car, a '65 Volkswagen Bug, orange in hue, lay upside down on the rocks. The soft contours of its shell were gone. The round top, for instance, was flat. On the driver's side the door had fallen open and hung off the hinges. It must have crinkled up real fast, I thought, squinting down at a thousand diamonds on the bank, at the steering wheel, the gear shift, the boulders. If I had my kaleidoscope glasses then I could have looked through them, refracting the discolored seat, confusing the bag of oranges that rolled out of a grocery bag in the back. Yes, I would have liked my glasses. As it stood, the details struck with impossible clarity. Each shade, each sound, the bird's hoarse tongue. Red plastic rope lashed around the broken railing. Nothing twisted about my vision, just a scene where once there was a song.

The camera hangs on a hook behind tomorrow's clothes for work. I imagine it there, odd square extension. I imagine what it's like on the good days, when I'm sharp enough to keep up with life. What is that element that I can't catch by trying? Maybe I should try, on a day like today.

Neither I nor the camera move. I lie in bed, willing things to happen. The robbery of my job turns out to be what happens to my head after five o'clock. When I drove home tonight I heard a funny noise in the engine, a squealing. I pulled over to the right-hand lane, my ears full of pressure. Reaching for the emergency flashers, slamming on the brakes, I realized nothing was wrong. Maybe it was another car. My heartbeat started subsiding.

Along Commercial Street I walked, head held high. It was here my career as a shoplifter took shape. I flung my hair behind my shoulders and narrowed down my eyes. Untouched and unsmiling, I maneuvered through the summer crowds. I had a mission. Certain things in the shops: certain small things. Things that fit in a pocket or a bag. First it was rock candy. Then, a red, white and blue tube top. Paperbacks, jewelry, pink and green striped socks. Makeup, moisturizer, a windup clock. I came to town in the morning and asked for a bag. By midafternoon I went home, bag full, and bound up the stairs in the cool, dark house. In my room, I took off my sneakers and emptied out the sand on the wooden floor. I lined up the objects between Carrie's bed and mine. Carefully I wrote the prices of everything on a little yellow pad. Then I put it all back in the bag.

His wasn't an ordinary bookstore, no. Bathed in light it was, beaming.

✶

Carrie writes, from Saint Louis:

*You got Grandma's invitation, of course. I'm not going. I can't.
I just can't miss this convention in Chicago. But you really should
go. One of us has to . . .*

*Bob and I are going on a cruise this fall! To Bermuda! The
company's paying for it. So, how's your new job? Are they letting
you do any photography, as you had hoped?*

Fancy linen, white and shining, was spread across Grandmother's
table. She had put out all her silver, even thimbles and candle-
snuffers, in a long crooked row. In ten years I hadn't missed her
hawkish voice, and no one can tell me she looks like my mother.
A miracle, anyway, that I came at all. Hadn't met *him* until that
day and it didn't matter. He was a card champ. Along the Eastern
seaboard. Later they moved to Florida and salamanders crawled
across their table.

I came by bus. Passing through towns without names, I struck
up a conversation with the man on my left, a philosopher, sad and
foreign. I fancied he was French, what did I know? His dark hair
slid back in waves as a movie actor's might. The blue cardigan
sweater he wore moved me. Looking out at the whipped landscape
he whispered, small bitter orange pits his words: "I don't like this
country." My mind worked, but I had nothing to say. Around Boston, I pretended to go to sleep, and after a while, I did.

I woke with the tires grinding to a halt. The bus stopped in front
of a coffee shop, the Greyhound station. Frantic suddenly, my hair
a mess, I zipped up my bags and stuffed my shirttail down my
pants.

I came in from the rain, to his shop. BOOKS it said in the window,
on the second floor. A bold handpainted sign. I opened the door at
the top of the stairs slowly. Bookshelves lined the walls, and two

bookcases with glass doors stood in the middle of the room. He sat at a desk by the window, eating a sandwich. His feet were up. He looked from the window to me and started chewing.

He was old and I was young: I kept my eyes on the books. Slowly I realized they were all about sex. They had titles like *Long Years in Tangential India, Lagoon Truth, Sky-crier and Baboon, Just Now, In Death, In Love, In Position, Candledark, Crustfinger, Zipper Stories, When It's Over, Delta's Passage Over the Moon, Pyramid Love, Phoenix: Crow Bird, Blunt Sliding, Liver Skin, Dozens of Attractive Options.*

I suspected they were old and wise, and I trailed my fingers over the unyielding bindings as if they were grass. Tick, tick, tick. A whole section in Japanese, another in Hebrew and Greek and Christ, I didn't know these languages but the characters, the letters, cried out to me and I longed to linger. Aztec, surely, Mayan —I trailed my fingers over the glass case preventing me access to the splendorous black books: no names or titles. I pressed my palm against the cool glass and felt my perspiration stick.

Pulling my hand away, I continued walking the circle that began and ended at that desk. His sandwich, so foul. When I got there I had a better look. He wasn't Norman Mailer, of course. Norman I have never met. But he was as close to Norman Mailer as you can get. I stood there and watched.

What's in the cage, Norman?"

"Matilda," he said, "Roon roon."

Pivoting in my short step forward I looked. A cage gilded as noontime only no light shone here, no ordinary light. Then why was it shining with a strange untoward gleam?

Matilda: dusty yellow feathers, large for a canary, clipped of wing. She was staring at the mirror, oval and clean. The thin branches of her cage swung when she swung. She's not real. She's an illusion, I thought. So I looked back at his face, at the books.

"How much are they, usually?"

"Birds?"

123

"Books. These."

"No price is fixed, but show me what you want and we'll arrive at a solution."

"The black books, how much are they?"

"Ah, the black books."

On the desk, in white wax wrap, nested his half-sandwich. A book, bent at its spine, was folded downward. Besides that the desk was empty, clean, scant, smooth. A place to lie on? Norman, or the man in the room, sat behind the desk but then he stood. He was taller than I had thought. He pulled at his belt obscenely and walked toward the cabinet.

Have I told you about my room? When I lie in bed the corners cobweb in and darken. I'm faced with a five-and-dime portrait of space. I'd like to have a conversation, but my apartment-mates are fucking in the next room, and my car makes a funny noise so I won't drive it at night.

His fingers were long but his hands were crumpled. The crust outside his skin, on his skull, his face, his chest, could be zipped off, down the middle, and out would step a delicate man with olive skin, a mane of thick goosey hair and the best hips.

Hamburgers fried in a skillet until the outsides were black, string beans with the ends cut off by me (lined up in rows of five, then chopped), frozen french fries. This was dinner on the nights they went out. Carrie and I in the kitchen, and the babysitter on her way. They went out, you see, Mom and Dad, all dressed up, his face smooth and soft, her perfume wrenching. In a hurry, they were gone. Gave us kisses on the lips. Ate french fries from our plates. Told us they wouldn't be out too late.

I always woke up when their bedroom light went on, when the water rushed in the bathroom sink. Both of them came in to kiss me good night. Don't you see? Don't you see?

✳

The loops lash around my chest in big white bands, guilt and desire both hold an end. My chest is compressed, my breath ever shortened. A hand of unknown origin, the sum of every moment I've passed, fingers my neck. Marionette, puppet, automaton. I am all of these. It takes so long to see you are a slave.

Feel me tugging listlessly at your belt. Consider me a passing stranger. Look at me from the side, in reflection. Disrupt my access to your eyes and you have killed me. So I died. What isn't a lie? At some point the walk goes on forever. In brilliant sunshine I sweat, and the lies I've told myself lose their shine.

Oh Norman, what do you make of me? I am your spirit, your shadow, I climb trees too. I guess I'll have to write a dictionary, a thesaurus, a table of contents, to guide you. Until then, though, I'll spend time with you, rolling skin against skin, blueness on blue. The lights will be bright in my library. I want to ride with you.

My mother of the sheet tent, Saturday morning. Dad out doing something, the radio is on. Singing songs together, I had a beautiful voice then. It is raining outside and the window holds us in, in this warm place, as old as an old sock, as fetid as the back of a drawer, as charged as silk. Already I have watched cartoons on TV, then I woke them up. Mom smokes in bed; she laughs huskily. The lights are off and the room lingers in the still light of the day. Singing, then, and snuggling under her arm. At once, I dive under the sheets. I tickle her feet, I try to, but she moves them hastily, laughing. She moves them hastily but gently, too, because I'm there. As I come up from under the covers I smell something familiar, an animal I have smelled before. I slide up and sit correctly, leaning on the headboard. She is a stranger to me. Her large white underwear, shoes with thick high heels, jars of medicine and pills. She says I must go, she is going to dress. I leave and fifteen years later, while toweling dry after a winter shower, I smell the animal again, only it's me this time, not my mother.

How can I express a death that isn't even permanent, let alone romantic? It hums a constant reproach; it leaves your mouth tasting foul, your ears clogged, your eyebrows furrowed into great steely knots. You choose it (somehow) and tell your friends that you like it. It pays you money: every other week you are alarmed and sickened by the slight amount. This is the death I lead. I'm good at it.

I heard the conversations from my bedroom, where I lay above the sheets, limbs stretched in all directions. Grandmother must have called every night, every day, every minute the phone was ringing and Dad would intone: "It's your mother." Then her voice, at first quiet, resigned, kind.

I looked for her and didn't see her, I saw her and didn't look for her. Even in my hatefulness I recognized a girlish glamour on her side of the couch.

Your father must know what happened. Your father could tell you what went wrong.

I stood before her tall and awkward, like Gulliver, without control.

She got up and embraced me hard for an old lady.

"Nona, my wedding will be complete with you here. Please meet Gunn, my darling."

He filled out the tuxedo well for someone his age, maybe seventy.

"I know how much this means to Vanny. It's so good to meet you at last."

Vanny, Vanessa Bowle, wore a print dress, tiny flowers like spiders all up the front. Her kiss stung.

I said, "Likewise."

In the bathroom I checked my teeth, sharp and strong. Washing my hands I tried to keep my eyes from the little porcelain poodle, but eventually I couldn't. A blue glazed dog. I had given it to her.

After the ceremony, I sat outside with a distant cousin on the porch. Card tricks entertained the elders inside. I had drunk so many bourbons I didn't taste them anymore.

"Did you know they played strip poker?" I asked my born-again cousin.

"No, I didn't."

"They do, you know. At night. They sit out here on the porch in rockers and drink a few of these, then, when they're nice and loose, he says something like, 'How 'bout a hand?' and she knows just what he means. He's better than she is, you understand, but he lets her have a few, maybe so he's down to his pants and shoes, then—"

"How do you know all this?"

"What?"

"I'm going in."

This is my movie, the one I'll make, when I have a little time:

Young woman of twenty or so. Locked in attic by evil minister/father. Denied pen and paper. Mother cuts off her long hair. Months go by. Young woman washes her face every morning, holding back the hair that is no longer there. She stares out the window and watches stray cats, one especially, a white one. Her evil brother runs the cat over with his Jeep. The young woman begins to lose her eyesight, she virtually goes blind with despair. The world fades out. Fade-out. What do you think?

She led us into the kitchen. The room smelled of life lived under glass. I've never felt more like a laboratory rat. African violets everywhere, all in menacing bloom.

"Sit down, have some juice."

On the kitchen table a crystal pitcher of red liquid sat as if it had been waiting there, still and lifeless, for years. Beside it, a plate of cookies, ugly Grandmother cookies, gathered dust. Carrie and I slid onto our seats. The old woman poured the juice.

Leaning back on the kitchen counter, she clutched our jackets to her body with wooden arms as if they were ransom. I swallowed the warm red punch. Grandmother just stared.

"Why are you looking at us like that?" my sister rudely asked.

"Carrie," I hissed.

Grandmother said, "I'll go put these away."

On the way up from Cape Cod all Carrie did was complain. Dad already looked unhappy, and she was only making things worse. I hit her—softly—to make her stop. She shrieked, of course, and Dad yelled, "That's enough!" Now she poured the contents of her glass back into the pitcher. It made a sad, hollow sound. I didn't hate her so much anymore.

I never say yes to anything. I never look you in the eye. My words are not even like crabs, that eventually get there. More like water beetles, or crickets. Apparently moving in one direction and then, without warning, heading off in another. I try to train myself to look forward, act evenly and easily and in a direction. But looking in your eyes is like being on an open fire.

I asked her if I could water the plants and she said yes. The watering can had a long, curving snout. I approached the first African violet warily, and then grew bold, watering all the plants in the kitchen, one by one. I ventured into the living room. More plants here in violent bloom (was this all that lived in a house of deathly calm?). I walked and hummed a cracked tune. Quietly, fragmented, not really happy. And I looked around again. I saw closed doors. I opened one. As the light fell into the dark room, I saw them. The pictures. Portraits of my mother, all lined up against the wall. Unfinished, half-done, abandoned. In each her eyes tortured and her smile bare. The watering can dropped, water spilled on the floor. I heard Grandmother's voice carry through the walls:

"Nona? Nona? Where are you?" When she came in the living room, I closed the door and turned around. She looked at me. I looked at her.

"Come into the kitchen. Play some cards."

Daughter.

Lungs, throat, mouth, filling with water. Same tongue that knew all the words to all the songs, lolling. Empty and alone. How could everyone be so cruel? If it was her idea, if it was God's idea, if Dad, if Grandmother—

A stone. I am a stone. No water can fill me. Either I am whole, or I am ground down. But no one can push anything into me. I am hard, ground, cold, stone.

I sat on the pier and my heart hummed with the *accident*. Everything, I saw, could be misplaced. My ringless fingers rubbed away at the wood, against the grain.

You ask me to describe my father and I say, I can only circle him. Before she died he was brilliant and beautiful. He built us dollhouses and gave puppet shows and sang us to sleep. They kissed like mad lovers on the porch, under the light. He sang. He danced. He ate, slept, wrote, ran, argued, got up, played violin. We four. We could do anything.

Beanstalk. I was once a beanstalk to be snapped in spring. Then I became a mystery, even to myself. I became someone wearing a trench coat in a cornfield in drizzle at five o'clock. Crows flew in three directions. It was Halloween.

You are the smell of eucalyptus on my fingers. You are an inlet, to the ocean. I swim in clear water and can see the bottom. Rocks and tendrils. I am a small trout. You are an atmosphere, an element, a mobility. When I am with you fins grow, I drop my

129

briefcase, my fidgeting hands steady.

She pulled me aside in the morning, after ten years.

"I know you didn't care about this wedding. And I know you think you hate me. But let me just tell you one thing, something you didn't know. I blamed your father but I could have blamed myself, or anyone. I never believed it was an accident. No. No accidents. Before you could say my name, or your own name for that matter, we went to Spain, all of us, do you remember?"

I reached a destination I hadn't been headed for. Just another gray day. The vagueness and lack of character that comes from walking death (so popular). Raining in the morning, a little clear that afternoon. The small of my back told me it was time for tea and cookies. Instead I rounded a corner. Blocks, signs with squared edges, streets all going one way and symmetrical tiles on the walk. Then I crossed the bend, I came to it, a store. A flower shop, a bookseller, a jewelry store, a Roman forum, a theater, a doctor's office, a bedroom. You should have seen how the frame slid all exultant around the door, like an ebony constrictor. So I placed my hand on the knob and pulled, like Alice in Wonderland, Dorothy in Oz. And every convention in the world ripped off of me, fell down on me like confetti, like an earth-sized piñata. You want to know what happened then?

I never had a mother. I had a father once. My mother killed herself when I was young, when she was young. At a bullfight, she ran into the ring and kissed the toreador's feet. My father became angry and slept in the next room that night. But Mom didn't sleep at all. She walked along the shore in darkness, her feet on cold ground, her head in the starry air.

And so it happened that we, two daughters and he, spent evenings at the table, eating dinner. Silence, damn it, and salt and pepper.

Now I remember how Carrie and I looked at him from the side, hoping for an element that wasn't there. How he every night for a million years carefully cut up his steak and spooned a second helping of rice onto his plate. Now I remember our vicious little eyes, transfixed. He just ate. He ate and ate and ate. All those nights, and the hope we held out for. For once, maybe, we wanted laughter. Or tears. We looked and listened, but no words came. He spelled it out so carefully: we have no love here. Every night we did the dishes and gave him a kiss on the cheek and then he'd read in his chair under the stand-up lamp with the pull chain. Carrie and I watched *Star Trek* and did our homework, and he just sat there. Some nights he left the house after we were in bed. Left the house. We heard the door.

So when Norman said, Fuck me, I looked into his bored eyeballs and said, Where? On the deck of my boat, it's cold there. Salt, brine and plastic. He kissed my clothes. He ripped my legs open. His penis had the length and breadth of history. He held me by the hair. I could have done something had I not been pinned to the surface of the ocean, and had I cared.

The next day I went back to the store.

"It didn't have to be like that," I said.

"Like what?"

"You didn't look at me."

"What is there to see?"

On the way home I felt puzzled, like a stage trick in a magician's show, the woman cut in two. My feet did the little dance on one side, and my mouth hung open on the other. Every step was a kind of nightmare, because I knew why I was walking. It was my car again. Couldn't be driven. Only now I wanted to be driving it. Because if I crashed I knew that something would remember me. That the dents in the fence would be my name. And that would be better than this drowning, in the hard air.

131

✳

A rum and Coke. Another.

Dear Mom: Did someone fuck you on the deck of his boat? Did no one understand when you kissed his feet, not me, not Dad, not your mother? Did you walk in dark circles in your head, and the longer it went on, the smaller, the smaller, until you were jumping up and down and wrapping yourself tighter and tighter like a horse with his foot in a noose, did you falter?

I think you can just kill yourself, Grandmother. Like the rest of us. Don't paint a mystery when you're the butler.

Over the trees. The plane tilts, and I see. Great quilted pastures of olive and wheat, red roofs and dirt roads and it's all so familiar. Completely sure I'll die landing, I don't care. Life has swung open like a front door.

The arena is filled with blue hats and yellow nets. Women throw themselves out of the air like scarlet blossoms. When they land, the sand is rockier than they remember. Running in the hot sun, blinded and young. The red cape. A body firm and strong. Pompous and romantic and wan. Running headlong, into the end.

Matilda

She said: I've come across a new map of the world, pear-shaped and brownish blue. The countries are burnished gold, and their shapes change in the light. There is one road, a scarlet chasm, and it cuts through the land like a lightning streak.

I miss our conversations. As I stand in line, I imagine tossing that globe up and down, revolving and revolting in my hand. I imagine you will be at the island's port to greet me, Matilda, in a pleated silk skirt and a sensible paisley blouse, calves strong and unstockinged over patent-leather shoes. You will embrace me and save me from my life.

When I first spoke, she wasn't listening. She listened to her Walkman, clutching a book on Egyptians and staring down. We were on a sidewalk, waiting for a bus. I recognized her from long ago. I said hi when she looked up. She smiled bleakly and turned her back.

Dear Matilda, I loved you instantly but you didn't know me at all. I felt alone then and ashamed of my shoes.

She said: I'll be reincarnated, of course. If I'm lucky, my legs and hips will be rich brown dirt for dogs to dig in and roots to find water through, and maybe my soul, the airy part, will be a bird, like that one, a robin. And I'll know how to fly, finally.

She laughed. She shuffled to the door in her socks and slid down the hall.

At the dinner table, she leaned toward me, one arm on the table, the other in the air, holding a cigarette by her ear. She told me a secret, and as she spoke she cocked one shoulder forward and smiled. She is a bony, fragile thing, I thought. Her neck is thin, and she doesn't know her own beauty. I became immensely worried she didn't eat enough, that she needed someone to feed her cake. I could be that someone, offering mouthfuls of lemon meringue and strawberry shortcake and poppy seed and mocha by the heaping forkful—big wedges of cake, every afternoon. It would be me, at the hospital bed, whispering back, yes, yes, yes, and filling her with creamy frosting and cakes, cake upon cake, until she was happy. Dear God, if she'd only let me.

Dear Matilda, the ferry hasn't even left the mainland, and here I am, writing you! Why, why didn't you call? I spent these last few days in a nervous frenzy, paranoid at the bank, the post office, the hair salon. What is it to me, my new straw hat, if you don't see me in it? How lonely my selection of books, old and hard. That you didn't answer your phone, no messages, no address, no plans—no us. You of the Grecian sweaters, claptrap briefcase and saintly smile. I am as lonely as my suitcase, all shut up.

I knew your name long before I met you. And I knew what it would be like to lie around in the living room, watching you think. In most cases minds are sealed shut to me, but not yours. Your brain is a strange jewel, and I treasure it, and don't know it, as I treasure and don't know the day I turned ten.

She said: You are what you do. What are you?

I saw us as an open window in summertime. Afternoon sun sprawling on the bed, the nightstand, our unmade plans. Our secrets danced together in a light bulb, sliding up and down in the silvery glass, undiscovered. You gave me yourself when I needed such a thing, I was the body, you the Holy Ghost. My days were spent cowed behind a desk, eager to compromise my once-in-a-lifetime life for pocket change. Like a brilliant murderer, you broke the chain.

I sat on the left, you on the right. We drank fresh lemonade. Our lawn chairs were wet and moldy from a winter in the cellar, it was still too early, really, to take them out at all. In the distance, we saw the sea. We didn't talk, we listened—with such acuity that when we went in for the night it was all I could do to stop trembling. With steady patience I watched TV, leaching out the splendor.

The men sitting across from me on the ferry remind me of you. One, he's pure animal: sixteen, swarthy, mute. Beside him, a man without a wedding ring, with calm blue eyes turned up, holding a hat to his lap with cool fingers. Something about the two of them gives me a start, and I'm eager to get on with things, even if it means being away from you.

The ferryman's whistle pulls me further out to sea. The ocean expands around me. It is the steel blue of her eyes, and all is calm on all sides. I look in front of me with anticipation, loss and need. Slowly the sea air fills me, tears wet my eyes.

She said: You are in love with the streets that separate us, the oxygen that makes us sleep.

She conducts her life like an orchestra. I am the audience, of one. Fickle, detached, she turns on the cold water. She says she'll never be a mother. I believe her.

Stepping up to the door of the bungalow, a place of retreat, I hesitate. In one hand I carry my typewriter, a straw hat, sunglasses. In the other, a suitcase, a willow cane, and the keys. It's nearly sunset. Down the street I hear a child laughing. Above me the telephone cables cross haphazardly, and birds, too dark to mention, hover by the trees. Some succulent white blossoms tumble toward me, moths shine in a circle of light by the door. In a moment, the night breeze may be chilly. Earlier it was too warm. But now, feeling the grim intoxication of the keys in my hand, I know it's all because of you. In the black bushes and the wooden steeple before me is the silence of your phone these two days past. It's the hug I never received. I'll open the door now, and set down my things, and by the light of my solitude, I'll write to you of the worth in an empty blue bottle on a sill, of the flash of the neighbors' TV, and of silence, the blues, yellows, and reds of it, which if you had held me, and made me yours like I wanted to be, I wouldn't see.

Look at the Moon

"What's wrong now?" the therapist asks.

Samantha is a magazine on the couch: colorful, well-edited, folded over.

"It seems nothing has gone wrong in my life, Bob, that's the problem. I was hoping to have had some minor childhood trauma, I even had the man picked out, that tall, red-haired friend of my father—that would explain my aversion to red-haired men—but nothing has surfaced there. What's the point? Should we try hypnosis again?"

"It's up to you, Samantha. I have some time next Tuesday afternoon for a long session, and of course the rate is doubled per hour."

"Of course, you have that much more of my unconscious to work with when I'm under."

The therapist looks like her father, and mother. He looks like her brother, professor and the girl in nursery school who punched and broke her tiny bean-shaped nose. Samantha thinks for a moment of her sex life. *That* is what's important here. But sex for Samantha is watery as a desert mirage. Where's the thirsty traveler?

"Do I look different when I'm under hypnosis?" she coyly asks.

"How do you think you might look?" responds the therapist, stifling a yawn.

Samantha thinks: I might look like Ingrid Bergman, or Tess of the d'Urbervilles. She uncrosses and recrosses her legs, exposing, remembering, and re-covering a run in her stocking. She looks out the window. Oh, to be a bird!

Writing the check, her hand trembles. She is sorry to leave the therapist, to whom she has just told a dream. She feels that paying for this experience cheapens it. She now wishes she hadn't mentioned the dream at all. *For the favor of an ear*, she writes in the memorandum section. She smiles at the therapist's crotch on her way to the door.

Samantha sits on a stool at the diner. Lawyers come here. She leans toward them in an effort to hear. Jail terms: they fascinate her. She spoons in ice cream, meditating on the numbers: one month, eight months, three hundred years. The man down the counter is blowing his nose over and over. Victim of a romantic disaster? Perhaps he needs a friend, someone to talk to. Samantha imagines the Eiffel Tower, marble tables, heads bent together under an umbrella. And then the law reaches her through the other ear. You would never find Samantha in jail. Never, never, never.

Samantha sits in her apartment and stares at the walls. She's got a closet full of clothes, stained and threadbare. Lined up in a neat row, her misshapen shoes conjure up the Depression era. Pictures from magazines smugly stare out from Plexiglass frames; these photos of faraway places are centered on each white wall. Yes, Samantha is a good and happy girl, and she is wearing her white sweater, buttoned up to the neck, and her ankles are bound, or crossed, at the ankles.

"Hello?" she says anxiously after the phone rings once and she's leapt from catatonia to quick, hopeful attention. Perhaps it is a secret admirer.

"Grandma, how nice of you to call!"

Samantha surveys her room, in her mind putting away any incriminating evidence, the paraphernalia of a life rejected by the church. Samantha will ferret out any sign of sloth, or pleasure for its own sake—other than small pleasures, of course, pleasures so mean that to enjoy them one also wants to commit suicide on the spot. No, her apartment from this angle appears convincingly ascetic—only don't look at the bed, hard and flat, covered with a natty, practical throw, even the pillows seemingly sewn to the mattress, as if to prevent spontaneous reactions. Looking at that bed too long would turn even a confirmed Catholic girl into a slut.

Samantha fingers the crucifix around her neck: the old woman gave it to her for Confirmation fifteen or twenty years back. There is the tiniest pinpoint of a diamond in the middle, craftily embedded in a chiseled mirror. Samantha likes the diamond, and always thinks of it as the size it pretends to be. She never once considered the cross just a cheap piece of metal.

What could her grandmother be calling for? To inquire about her health? What should she tell her?

The crucifix-giver has forgotten Samantha's address. She wants to send her a birthday present, which means, as it does every year, a card and five dollars.

Samantha flips through her address book, buoyed by lust. Her fingers stop at one name, one Mark Braun. It is Thursday night, well into the dinner hour. Surely she could be calling to reminisce, as civilized people do.

Mark Braun was her junior high paramour, a boy who first impressed Samantha by walking down the school hall with his butt in the air, leaning on a field hockey stick and calling himself a constipated gym teacher. It's a stretch. Still, there is the glamour (or the hunger) that makes calling a man, even one whose dusty, crinkled condom package she's picked up off the assembly hall floor, a viable alternative to another early night alone in the arms of her monkish bedcovers. Samantha picks up the phone and dials.

Yes. It is a yes. Before she knows it, Samantha is dressed for Saturday night. She's bought new, violet-colored contact lenses for the occasion. She wears her "Brattleby: the Heart of Connecticut" T-shirt. Cupid's arrows have struck.

At the bar, Samantha gobbles peanuts. She avoids making eye contact with herself in the mirror. But as the hour approaches for Mark to meet her here, her heart grows colder and colder. She is disgusted. Why did she call him after all these years? He never really meant anything to her. Now she has made the impression, before even meeting, that she cares.

Entering the bar, Mark Braun looks peevish in a tight-fitting ski jacket and slim loafers. His hair is combed back into a precise shape, wrapping his skull like banana peels. The combination of self-consciousness and suavity is remarkable, poignant even. Samantha, in spite of her reluctance, decides to go whole hog.

"I wanted to tell you in all honesty," she begins, "I've had some problems in my life, with men, women, whatever. I've always wanted to tell my secrets to someone, and there's something about you, I feel I could tell you. But where should I begin? I had a dream the other night. There was a woman in it who was very fat, and her skin wasn't hard, it was spongy. She opened a closet door and inside was an Easter basket filled with rancid eggs, the shells painted with pastoral scenes and bunny rabbits. The woman—don't know who she was exactly—put her hand to her mouth and started eating her own fingers."

Samantha laughs nervously. Mark laughs nervously—very nervously. Remembering her manners, Samantha asks:

"But what about you? Do you still wear a blue overcoat?"

"An overcoat . . . yeah. I'm in corporate marketing now. I'm taking a class at Yale this semester. I still live with my mother."

"Fascinating!" Samantha says in a booming voice. Some teacher with pink lathery hands once told her if you have nothing to say, at least say it loudly.

"I remember your mother," she continues. "She didn't seem to like you very much. She was always yelling at you. I remember what she did that time you wet your pants. You had to clean them out in the kitchen sink. Latisha and Max and I waited in your room."

"I don't know if that was me . . . I don't remember that."

"Well, you always were clever. Shall I tell you? I still love you!"

Mark has a consternated, perhaps even constipated, look on his face. Maybe he doesn't appreciate her offensive line of action: it must be hard to warm up to a torpedo. Not that he couldn't seduce her—oh no, Mark knows how to make the moves on any girl. He must have had five women, at least. Samantha can see it all now. The conquistador and his soon-to-be-conquered señorita sitting on a couch together. Mark edging over, an inch at a time: one inch when he gets up to change TV channels, one inch when he examines her lovely earring (did she get that from her mother?), one inch—the final one—with no explanation at all. It's hard to know whether to exhale or inhale when approaching a woman. Should you have just taken a slug of beer, so that lukewarm smell dominates the air space? Should you have lit a cigarette, or just put one out? Should you go to the bathroom first? But that might seem like too much planning. Mark has surely learned to add some spontaneity to the process. You've got to watch *her* for cues. When she extends her arms, stretching, yawning and saying, "Oh, I'm so tired," it's a good time to move forward.

"Love, huh?" Mark says at the bar, swilling his beer.

Samantha peers at Mark's glimmering forehead. He looks charming in the semidarkness. Aloud, she muses:

"Over the years things have been funny in terms of boyfriends. I've had my heart broken a few times. I've been in love with the most garlicky individuals. In fact, I have a fascination with the mediocre. I love gas station attendants, better yet, the unemployed. I love men who have rat's nests for hair and murderous intentions. There's something about a man who hasn't taken a shower in days . . . primal. I like a man who doesn't require any stupid preliminaries. It's just me and you, babe. I love a man who seems to be winking at the waitress, making a phone call when I go to the ladies' room. But sometimes it's hard to find a balance. My therapist—oh, did I tell you I'm in therapy? Isn't everyone?" Nervous laughter, again, from Samantha, rejoined by Mark's fixed grin. "A balance, it's hard to—"

"Can I just tell you something?" Mark interrupts. "You have a beautiful nose. So why don't you relax? You're a little anxious, it seems. Finish your drink. You haven't touched it. Go ahead. I'll be right back, OK? I'm going to the men's room."

Samantha doesn't have a beautiful nose, that should have been the tip-off. She blinks her newly violet eyes.

"Sure," she says, a purr of a sure.

She waits at the bar, chin in hands. Samantha Braun, Ms. Braun, Mrs. Mark Braun, Samantha Brown Braun. Mark seems, clearly, to understand her. She has never felt so—frank, so forward. At last! She's discovered the secret of romantic union. She knows she can say *anything* to the right man.

Samantha's gin and tonic has turned into a tepid lake. The ice cubes have gone back to their mother, water, and the tonic has given up its captive princess, air. Only the gin remains poised for action. Samantha taps her freshly manicured fingernails on the bar. That Mark—constipated after all?

She begins watching the door with the stick figure on it. Men, hoisting their pants, tugging their underwear, realigning their belts, come lumbering out like immigrants from an underwater country. Samantha is getting irritated. Just finish your business while you're in there!

The bartender has already wiped up the bar in front of Mark's stool. Samantha stops watching the bathroom door. How could a person leave in the middle of a conversation like that? How uncouth, unsatisfactory. Perhaps he was raped and murdered in the stall, a crowbar denting his mastodon forehead. Perhaps a huge lizard has him pinned to the toilet and strips him away, limb by limb. Giving the bartender a generous tip, Samantha leaves in the guise of a martyr.

Samantha practices the clerical arts and crafts at a publishing company in midtown Manhattan. She lives in a pink, semicircular enclosure in the front hall. As the editors pass by, she chimes "Good morning" to their trail of ambrosial perfume and coffee aromas, then she turns back to the newspaper. A for actuarial assistant, B for busboy, C for clerk. It is time for a new job, she's determined, having gotten over her original torpor. She has a college degree after all—she knows how to paint, dance, write poetry, critique literature. Surely there is something better than reception for her. Receiving what? She's not feeling it. But Samantha becomes bored with the job listings and turns to the personals.

"The phone's ringing, love," her boss sings, passing by Samantha's Pepto-Bismol universe.

"Got it," she smiles.

She lets the little red lights blink like fish eyes and gets back to the paper.

Bisexual white male desires fun-loving couple for good times, willing to travel.

Could he be her cowboy? Somehow it seems unlikely. The man Samantha's after would shoot another mammal if it came too close to his one-woman lair.

Male, 40s, good-looking, athletic, well-endowed, stable income, seeks beautiful lady for candlelight dinners, movies, walks across sunset-strewn Brooklyn Promenade.

Is that the description, short and faulty, of her dreamboat? No, too much gray flannel, too much Mark Braun here.

Incarcerated Scorpio, dies for poetry and rock and roll, remembers what it's like to be in love. Send pix.

Hmmm.

Samantha rereads this one: Chained lust, dark, deep, passionate, deadly, daring, understands her soul, is ready for reincarnation.

"Darling . . ." the boss chants on her return from the rest room, clumping by in fashionable shoes, "the phone, sweetie. . . ."

Samantha gets out a red pen and circles her man.

After work, Samantha walks around the city, making up errands. She will buy thread, she will get her shoes resoled, she will price witch hazel at various discount drug stores. On her way past the grocery store, she sees a little dog. At least she thinks it's a dog. It's a hairy animal of some sort, tied to a parking meter, over-bundled as a baby or a beggar in blankets and sweaters. Its dishrag neck is surrounded by a toothless rhinestone collar, black holes where the jewels once were. It (a dog, she's pretty sure) shakes tremendously, despite the garments. It stares at the entrance to the grocery store.

On her way back a few minutes later, the animal is still there, weak-kneed as ever, tail drawn between its legs with doglike attention to detail. Now it's looking around in some distress. It even looks at Samantha.

"Eek," Samantha responds. It's really a loathsome little creature.

But she pauses, having been singled out somehow. She peers down at the dog. It growls and wags its tail, both. There's one long tendril of gray hair on its hind leg, and it seems that by pulling the loose end, Samantha could unravel the dog altogether.

"Get away from my dog."

Samantha looks up. She is being addressed by a tall dog owner.

Big—young—movie star. Her jeans aren't completely secure, the top button is undone. Her belt hangs loose and long. She has an accent, too. She's a Transylvanian cowgirl.

"Oh, well. Your dog and I were just introducing each other. Say, haven't I seen you before? Weren't you a scuba diver in the south of France, picking tobacco from your tongue, men shivering around you in the sea air?"

"You and my dog? You the dog around here."

"Hold off a second. No fair."

Samantha shifts from foot to foot, facing the M. Monroe truck driver. The woman is sweating, but it is so cold! Too cold for anything but being at home, eating peppermints and orange slices and expounding on rodeos.

She leans over and unties her dog.

"Do you have a fever?"

The cowgirl flips her black hair out of her face, sending the metal objects that hang from her belt and shoulders into a flutter. Her boots are lengthy as she strides away from Samantha, the liberated dog trotting along at her side.

Samantha pushes and pulls at her finger joints as she hurries to catch up.

"It's a nice dog, I like dogs," Samantha says to the woman's back, formidable in black leather.

"What?" she asks, thinking she heard a response. Silence but for the city whoosh.

She continues: "I find dogs pleasing, and this particular dog most pleasing of all. Did you knit the sweaters yourself? Did you knit the dog?"

The animal turns around and gives Samantha a haughty look. Samantha slows down and watches the cowgirl's steps get lankier until she turns the corner.

Dear Box 499:

I've never been in jail myself, but I imagine it is very confining there. I know all about confinement, about energy that is stored. I'm no prude. I know how to have a good time. Really. I have a job, it's true. But inside I'm a panther.

I'm about five . . .

[Samantha stops writing for a minute, then scratches out that number.]

I'm very, very tall. I've got black hair and big boots and I walk down the street with giant steps, never looking backward.

Sincerely, Samantha Brown

P.S. No photo enclosed; photo shop gone bankrupt.

Samantha, job applicant par excellence, girl with a future, is on her way to an interview. The job is to write abstracts for a psychology newsletter. Her therapist suggested it to her during their last interlude, after hypnosis and before dinner. He feels she is attuned to the subject, it seems. In the elevator, Samantha stares at the fire detector: she knows it's a camera.

In the waiting room, phallic statues hover in the corners. Womblike couches recede under framed ink blots. Samantha stares out the window. The Twin Towers remind her of her mother; the Empire State Building, her father. Must be the air in this unit, she thinks, repressing an urge to smoke a cigar.

A woman in browns (Samantha thought brown indicated cancer) emerges from one of many closed doors and beckons her down a long hall.

The woman's office is small, square, windowless. She shuts the door. Too bad! Samantha slides uneasily into a chair.

"Do I know you from somewhere?" the woman asks, leaning over the desk, rolling out her words as if formulating an algebraic equation. Her hair is long and brown and dull. It sweeps over her brown turtleneck and brown wool vest like an opaque stocking.

"I don't think so," Samantha ventures.

"I read your sample. It was very good, though there were some grammatical problems."

Samantha had sent in a first-person piece on necrophobia; she burnt the edges of the paper so it looked duly somber.

"Well, yes, I have an instinctive sense of grammar and in the modern world instincts sometimes get shaded by intentions," Samantha explains. Her pink-fisted professor comes into view.

"I had a little trouble with the structure of the piece."

"The structure?"

"Exactly."

"I try to let things structure themselves, especially if they are of a psychological nature," Samantha shoots back with a smile. "I feel this adds, if not to the obvious clarity—"

"I thought your conclusions were hasty and personal."

"That's the best way to end everything, is it not?"

The woman, running her finger over the charcoaled edge of Samantha's essay, smiles benignly as an undiscovered virus.

"Naturally."

As the interview continues, the incredulousness of the gaze between the two women reaches unheard-of proportions. Psychology is a science, Samantha longs to cry. But it needs color, it needs fresh air!

They shake hands at the end of the half-hour with an understanding: both know they are repulsed by and uninterested in one another.

Samantha escapes onto the elevator.

On the tenth floor, a new passenger boards.

"What are you doing here?" Samantha asks Mark Braun.

"What are *you* doing here?" he responds, stabbing at the lobby button.

The door closes; the elevator doesn't move.

"Why, I was just at an interview," Samantha says. "This elevator isn't going anywhere."

"No shit," says Mark. He puts his vinyl briefcase on the floor and punches at that button once, twice, three times more.

"That wasn't very nice of you, last week, to leave me in the bar."

"Nice? Samantha, I'm sorry, but you've changed a lot since school."

"How so?"

"Instead of getting older, more mature, you've become younger."

"But I thought we were having a conversation and all. . . ."

Mark talks into the intercom: "Yes. We're stuck. Help. We need immediate help. We need to get out of here."

Mark takes off his jacket, folds it carefully around the railing and sits down on the floor. He takes some papers out of his brief-case and begins studying them, making use of his calculator.

Samantha is getting nervous.

"Mark?"

"What?"

"We could use this time to get to know each other better."

"That's OK, Samantha. I've got some work to do."

A few moments pass. Could this really be the same Mark Braun Samantha spent afternoons with, playing Release the Peddler? Could they have possibly thrown a ball to one another? She feels as if she's sifting through her photo album and seeing someone else's pictures.

"Mark?"

"What, Samantha?" he says, ticking off numbers.

"I don't think it's nice to leave someone in a bar. I don't think it's nice to sit there and do computer printout work while I'm standing here and we're stuck in this elevator together."

"Grow up."

"You grow up."

"Look, Samantha, you're not the only one who's had a hard life, not the only one who—"

The elevator has lurched and begun a smooth glide downward.

"Not the only one who what?" Samantha asks.

148

Mark scrambles to his feet.

"Forget it," he says, as the elevator opens. He's out the door like a Boy Scout's sling shot.

"I hate men, I hate men, I hate men," Samantha mutters, walking down the street on her way home. "I hate Mark, I hate Mark, I hate Mark."

The sun is on her shoulders but she doesn't feel it. She walks with her head down, watching the too-ugly sidewalk, the too-ugly street.

Maggie Cross walks in the sun. It burns her up. Her metal belts clank, her thigh-high boots glide effortlessly forward, her broken-wing black hair slips into her face.

Samantha doesn't even look up when a long and dark shadow passes over her body in a zigzag caress.

"I like dogs, too," she hears, in a familiar voice.

"What?" asks Samantha, looking back.

It's the cowgirl.

"I said, I think you're nice."

Samantha and Maggie sit at one of the bright places where people try to communicate. Samantha orders a soda; Maggie, black tea.

"Tell me about yourself," Maggie says gently. "What was your childhood like?"

"Me?" Samantha fidgets. Her dull story? Brattleby, New England's empty envelope?

"I'm from a nuclear family. Nuclear, in the sense of divorce—an explosion into the four great directions of the Holy Cross. My father went north. He went to a place where all his tears would dry up and he could wear winter coats. My mother went south. She fell in love with parrots and sunsets, now she's a child herself. Geoff, my little brother, went west, riding a quiet, meditative wave. And I, well, I went east."

"The divorce was troubling, I guess?"

149

"Not in the slightest. This is excellent ginger ale," says Samantha. "And what about yourself?"

Maggie looks ahead and stirs her tea blankly. It's cloudy over their café table suddenly, a rain shower is likely.

"I am willing to listen. I go to bars, a man drones on beside me: 'The snake bites and you have sixty seconds . . . the difference between volts and watts is. . . .' I know what he is going to say.

"There is a woman who sings on Wednesdays, only Wednesdays. Her voice pulls at me like a fish hook. What happens to her, I wonder, the rest of the week?

"The waitress sometimes tries to take away my things. My ashtray, my glass. I don't let her. You must have an object, like this," she clinks her teacup with a spoon. "This is the love story of the century."

Samantha of the suburbs leans forward, speechless. If a tidal wave came, she would stay seated at this table, watching Maggie speak.

Maggie drains her cup.

"Let's get together sometime, when the weather is better."

Yet it couldn't be brighter out.

The cowgirl gets up and leaves.

"Now what's the matter?" the therapist asks.

Samantha stares at the white ceiling.

"I remember when I was with my parents, we were walking on some grass . . . there were squirrels digging holes near the bushes. I had something on my nose. . . ."

"What were your parents doing?"

"I don't know."

"What do you think they were doing?"

"Digesting lunch, maybe. Discussing their tax return. But the squirrels . . ."

"Was your father wearing a clown outfit?"

"The squirrels—"

"Your father!"

"You don't care about the squirrels! You don't care about the seedpod on my nose!"

Samantha gets up off the couch. Bob smiles placidly behind his glasses.

"Come now," he cajoles.

"I'm never coming back! You never leave this room, how would you know about things that have no reason, no purpose, nothing!"

Samantha swings her purse across her shoulder with laudable drama and strides lengthily out the door into the noise-machined waiting room.

In her mailbox that week, on her birthday in fact, Samantha finds two items. One is in a blue, card-size envelope. The other is on cheap paper: prison stationery. She breathes faster.

Dear Samantha:

Thanks for the letter. You're right, jail is a drag. But someday I'm gonna get out of here. And then the world will see what I have in store. YOU CAN'T KEEP A GOOD MAN DOWN. You know what I mean, baby? Hey, in your next letter send a photo.

Keep up the faith. You sound like a beautiful girl.

Sincerely, Greg

Samantha rushes up to her apartment. She "sounds like a beautiful girl"! She is a sophisticated woman, corresponding with some sort of ax murderer.

When she's calmed herself from this moment of drama, Samantha sits down at her kitchen table cum desk cum ironing board and opens the other piece of mail, from the penny-pincher herself, Samantha's grandmother. As she suspected, it's a lovely card: a pastel of two horses in a flowery meadow, Abe Lincoln's face peeping out between blossoms. The horses have no feet. At

least, their hooves are only implied among the grasses. Samantha
sucks peppermints one after the other.

The phone rings. She jumps out of her chair.

"Hello?"

"Sabrina?"

"Sabrina?"

"What's your name?"

"Samantha?"

"Samantha, this is Maggie Cross, do you remember?"

A blackly clad female Zorro figure leaps before Samantha's
eyes.

"Sure, you have the dog."

"What are you doing now?"

"I'm, uh, reading."

"Could you meet me at Bill's Bar on East Sixth Street in half an
hour? It's important," the strange woman whispers.

"Sure, why?"

"Good," Maggie says, and hangs up.

Samantha puts down the phone. She pulls on her leopard-print
socks and heads out the door.

Bill's is dark and loathsome and Christmas decorations are up
even now, in February. Samantha tiptoes to the bar. She doesn't
see Maggie right away, but when she does, she notices a man is
with her. He looks like Darth Vader.

"Hi," squeaks Samantha.

The frightening people look over at her.

"Hi," Maggie says casually. "Dirk, this is Samantha."

Dirk looks down at Samantha from a penthouse apartment, fur-
nished by his hard head and cold glasses. He is pointy all over—
pointy boots, pointy ears, pointy nose. His pointy knees surround
Maggie's. She looks like a caught bird in his limb sculpture. He
snorts a hello and then proprietarily kisses Maggie's neck.

"Do you want a drink?" Maggie asks.

"OK, let's see, a screwdriver?"

Maggie orders the drink, paying for it with some money by one of Dirk's sharp corners.

Samantha cradles her cocktail. She is about to engage in some knowing banter when Maggie turns toward Dirk, and he puts his hands on her. Maggie begins to rock, slowly, back and forth.

Straightaway, Samantha knows she's somehow disorganized in her approach to this situation. Did she misinterpret Maggie on the phone? Perhaps she shouldn't have worn her white sweater.

"It's my birthday," she informs the intertwined skyscrapers.

No answer.

By midnight, Samantha has watched a preadolescent beat six contenders in pool. That boy shouldn't even be in a bar, Samantha considers, drinking through her swizzle straw. Dirk's hands move on Maggie's thighs while he argues politics and art with the bartender. Maggie's face is murderous and submissive as she rocks. She slips off her stool.

"Where are you going?" Samantha asks.

"To the bathroom."

"May I come?"

"Sure," Maggie scoffs.

In the ladies' room, Samantha sits on the sink while Maggie is in the stall.

"What's Dirk like?" she asks. "I haven't really gotten a feeling for him."

"He's the president of the United States. He's Picasso. He's Bonaparte. He's Mick Jagger. He's a horse. Is there any toilet paper out there?"

"Yes," Samantha leaps for the towels and hands some under the door.

"What do you like about him?"

Maggie has come out of the stall.

"Nothing at all."

Maggie's looking in the mirror.

"What's that?" Samantha says in alarm. Maggie has pulled her shirt to one side, she's observing her neck.

"What's the matter, haven't you seen blood before?"

At lunch the next day, Samantha is feeling a little insecure. She's having her authority-figure complex; this happens. Sometimes when she sees a policeman she has to stop herself from turning herself in. When her landlord calls, she is capable of slightly hysterical small talk: "Nice day, this is a nice building, you are nice, I like how clean the halls are, it's just a great city, don't you like this time of year?" Her boss's clunky shoes seemed monstrous all morning, capable of destroying her. Now, walking around in a stupor, Samantha wonders what to do. When feeling upbeat, she will shoplift during this hour. But today even that is beyond her. She makes plans to write a thank-you note to her grandmother.

On her way to the drug store to buy tissues for her bedside table, Samantha pauses in front of a church. She decides to go in. She sits in a pew and folds her hands. Sunlight, so pure outside, is sullied here by the blood of Christ. She sits in the shadows of the stained glass. She reflects on the black box in the corner, a nice little closet, modestly wrapped in fabric. She remembers that she has spurned her therapist. Her eyes wet at the thought. She gets up and goes into the curtained area of the confessional and sits down on a tiny bench. She hears a shuffling of paper on the other side of the screen—the sports pages? Details on the latest, most violent hockey mishap?

"Father?" she calls querulously.

"Yes?"

"I'd like to confess."

"Go ahead, my child."

"Is that all right? Is it the right time?"

"Go ahead, my child."

"Well . . ." What does she have to confess? What a world, what a life—nothing to confess. She's never killed, divorced or slighted anyone. When she is knocked over by a commuter on the subway platform, *she* apologizes.

"When I was little, I was mean to my brother."

"Go on."

This sounds familiar.

"We had a tree fort and I painted my name on it with big bold letters, and his with minuscule ones. Then I smeared the paint on his, too, so it was lost in a snowstorm, unreadable."

"That wasn't very thoughtful, my child."

"No, you're right," Samantha looks down at her lap. "It was awful, awful."

"But you repent?"

"Why, yes! Ever since, I've been perfect, like a perfect cloud on a perfectly cloudless day."

"That's all that matters. Go home and pray to God, and may the good Lord be with you always. Amen."

Samantha hears the shuffling of paper again.

"Is that it?"

"May God be with you."

On her way out, Samantha picks a quarter out of the dish by the Virgin Mary's feet; it'll go toward Kleenex for fits of nighttime melancholia.

Dear Grandma [cross out the name, pause, smile, squirm] Greg,

So, what did you do anyway—something brave and chilling, like Robin Hood? Are you a pirate? Did you rob someone of something important to her? Not that it matters—whatever you did, I'm sure you had to do it, I'm sure a passion just boiled up inside you and you couldn't control yourself. Losing control—it's such a pleasure.

I've been going to bars, especially Bill's Bar—do you know that one, on Sixth Street? Men find me spellbinding. I listen to long, sad songs and stare at the interior of my eyeballs. I'm exhausted from all the attention I receive from would-be lovers.

Well, I'll talk to you soon, I'm going to bed now, in black leather. . . .

Sincerely, Samantha

P.S. I've sent the film to be developed out-of-state. Should be included in next letter.

Samantha slips this missive into the red, white and blue box and twirls her crucifix around her finger.

Maggie calls on Thursday and asks Samantha to meet her at Astor Place after work.

When Samantha gets there, Maggie takes her by the arm without talking. She seems to have a destination in mind, but Samantha's questions in that regard have come to nothing. In fact, none of her conversational topics have hit a chord. Samantha can't tell if they are *amies* or if this is a kidnapping. The dog—named Stripe, Samantha discovers—looks less ragged today, but also less charming. He vies with Samantha for Maggie's side, nipping at Samantha's ankles when they stop at street corners. Samantha falls into silence and a distrust of dogs.

They continue walking until the streets narrow and the buildings slouch. Maggie keeps looking at her watch, cursing under her breath (Samantha thinks she's cursing the dog). She stops abruptly by a storefront, the window painted over in gray, the door dungeonlike in strength. What does Maggie do for a living? Samantha begins to wonder. Does she have a social security number?

Maggie ties up Stripe and approaches the door. Is this the end of the road?

"C'mon," Maggie says with annoyance, seeing Samantha's hesitation.

Samantha follows her inside. It isn't death! It's a hat shop.

A Tibetan man gets up from a chair in the back. He approaches them. He bows. Maggie knows him from before, it seems. They have a short conversation, and then he turns to Samantha. He begins to take hats down from infinite shelves, hats of silk and velvet and satin and fur. He puts them one after the other on Samantha's head.

"What's going on?" she stammers.

Maggie doesn't answer. She and the hat maker are making the decisions here. These hats are *War and Peace* gear, capable of deep-winter drama. Maggie shakes her head, shakes her head, shakes her head. When he puts one with a green satin ribbon and black fur on Samantha, Maggie says, "That's it," and pulls out her wallet.

"Maggie? What are you doing?"

"I'm buying you a hat. Happy birthday."

"But you don't have to do that," Samantha says, taking off the hat.

"Don't be stupid, Samantha."

Maggie's counting out hundred-dollar bills and handing them to the hat maker.

Samantha looks down at the hat. She puts it back on her head.

When she gets home, her answering machine is blinking. She listens to the message:

"Samantha, where are you? This is Dad. Your grandmother has died. The funeral is on Saturday. Call me as soon as you get in."

She takes the hat off again and it drops to the floor with a puff.

The funeral parlor is a medley of peach, mauve and ecru. A big picture of Our Savior splashes the wall with deeper color. Samantha's old aunts, ladies her grandmother's age, disappear into overstuffed chairs and couches, furtively glancing about, as if dodging Death's hardball pitches. The other relatives shuffle their feet on the echoing floor of the smoking room, laughing about odd matters. Samantha looks over at her brother standing in the corner. He could be the priest here, he looks so tranquil. Later she found out he was high on marijuana.

Samantha walks up to the coffin. No blood here. It's all very clean and color-coordinated. This is what she had wanted. A pretty death, with family.

Samantha looks at her grandmother's face.

"Oh, Grandma, it's all right about the five dollars, I swear."

Samantha walks down the streets of the Lower East Side the next day, looking for the store where Maggie took her. She has the hat in a bag. She will bring it back and return the money to Maggie. Why do I live the way I do, she wonders, wearing guilt like a poncho? She stares up at faces in windows, long underwear on clotheslines, gargoyles bloated with the years.

Crossing a street, she thinks she sees Maggie herself, holding a bakery box and standing in front of a door.

"Maggie?"

The woman turns around. It is Maggie. For once her hair is pulled back. Framed by a black band, her face is wide and pale as the moon. She looks frightened when she sees Samantha, but then she recovers.

"Hi, Samantha. I'm visiting someone," she says helplessly. Then, after a moment, "Do you want to come?"

They walk up three flights of light green, incoherent steps. The railing is drunk with disaster. When they get to a certain door, Maggie stops, drops the keys on the floor, picks them up again and unlocks the door.

"Hello?"

"Come in, come in, don't hesitate," a man's voice resonates from down a dark hall mapped with extension wires. There's a sickish gleam coming from the last doorway. It's not sunlight and it's not electric, either.

Samantha follows Maggie to the light and the voice.

Propped up in a hospital bed, an old man glares at them through a jumble of tubing, medical apparatus and quilts. His body looks almost nonexistent under the bedding, as if he is just a head, a pair of eyes staring forward.

"Hello, Daddy," Maggie says, leaning down toward the old man, kissing him.

"Lemon princess, clover lady."

"I've brought a friend, Samantha."

He levels his eyes at Samantha, paralyzed by the door.

"Come here."

Samantha walks forward; Maggie retreats to the wall.

"Sit down."

Samantha sits.

Still staring at Samantha, he says:

"Maggie, bird of paradise, sweet air of life and liberty, get us some refreshment? A scotch would do nicely."

"Now, Daddy."

"She's rather sweet, isn't she?" he answers.

Samantha has passed from anxiousness into a sort of lethargy.

Maggie leaves the room. Samantha has never seen her take such small steps before.

"Her parents are divorced and she's just lost her grandmother," Maggie chatters from the kitchen. "The grandmother was a source of consternation for Samantha, poor child. She's never been out of her own front yard, but she has a great sense of the possibility of pleasure. She imagines beauty as the coming together of opposites, some final geographic cataclysm."

Samantha shrugs foolishly at this rendering. The old man puts his cold, old hand on her young one.

"You'll do fine, plum, you have a nice sense of timing."

Maggie returns from the kitchen with a bottle and three glasses.

"You are a beauty after all," he says to her.

Maggie pours the drinks. She seems giddy; Samantha thinks

giddiness is odd on Maggie, the wrong color. Samantha tries to get up out of the chair by the man's bed, but Maggie holds her down by the shoulders.

"I'll toast to anyone who can tell a good lie or tell a fish from a cabbage," says Mr. Cross.

"Daddy . . ." Maggie coos.

They drink, Samantha taking a large swallow.

Later, when the man has fallen asleep, Samantha observes: "There's a rip in the carpet."

Maggie says: "He has read all the books in the apartment. He no longer likes to read, it smells too strongly of death, all those feelings on paper."

"Light comes through the tattered edges," murmurs Samantha.

"We came to this country when I was a girl, from Germany. The Krauses got on the boat and the Crosses got out. Mother was a masterpiece, so he tells me. I don't remember her at all. She left us on the dock, she left with a sailor. Daddy and I rode bicycles, we persevered. These hands," she turns them like grilling meat before Samantha, "were callused once, when he was young, and we worked together to build a home.

"In my dream I own a diner in the middle of the country. I put out the creamers. One morning the men come in with their rifles and their baseball caps and their checked flannel shirts. They've stooped to come in the front door. They look around for the creamers, but I haven't put them out yet. I am in a bunk bed in the back. I am naked and I can't get up. The men come in and see me there. They shoot me in the stomach, they tear the tight hide of my belly. They kill me because I didn't get the creamers. Then they go back outside to hunt for deer and the sweet cream of some woman. This dream has already happened."

Samantha looks from Maggie's face, marblelike in the dusky light, to that of her father. He smiles when he sleeps, like a child.

Maggie brushes the crumbs from the bedspread and brings the

empty glasses into the kitchen. Samantha reaches over to Mr. Cross's bedside table and steals a black and white photo of Maggie wearing a sweater.

Samantha wears the hat—she decided to keep it after all—to work the next day. Her boss calls it "vibrant."

Samantha says: "My grandmother died, and her face was pale as your stockings."

The boss smiles.

Midmorning, Samantha calls her therapist's office and hangs up when he says hello. She had thought of going to see him tomorrow for her regular appointment but then decided against it. After work, she writes a letter:

Dear Greg:

I bet you know how to build a fire with green leaves and moldy old twigs, even after a thundershower. I bet you get up at dawn to shoot a rabbit for dinner. In case you need a vision of the future, see the enclosed picture.

Yours, Samantha

"I've come about the job," Samantha informs the hustler/pimp/ manager behind the counter at a shoe store a couple of days later. It is Samantha's lunch hour. It is Valentine's Day. She's been flicking red envelopes vengefully into her boss's in-box all morning.

The man at the shoe store twists his mustache end. He runs his hand down his silk shirt, past the alligator- or maybe kangaroo-skin belt, and over the top of his linen pants, and then Samantha can't see his hand anymore.

"Do you have experience?" he asks.

"Lots."

She feels very, very small.

He studies Samantha. He moves his hand even further down,

161

and it emerges with a pad of application forms. He turns the pad so it faces her. He passes her a pen. The pen has a woman in a bathing suit inside it, and when Samantha turns the pen so she can write, the bathing suit peels off. By the time Samantha has finished writing her first name, the woman in the pen is fully undressed. Samantha plows ahead. Employment, education, possible prison record . . . she is having trouble seeing, having trouble getting the naked lady to fit between the lines, to do the job. But finally she is done. The man looks it over. As he does so, another woman emerges from the back of the store. She is wearing shoes that look like they've never been outdoors. She neither looks at Samantha nor the man. But he watches her, as if imagining sliding his manicured fingernails past the boundaries of her crotchless underwear. She walks slowly past them, past the racks of fabulous shoes, to the door. She looks out. She heaves a sigh. She turns around, the turn of a cheetah, and saturninely retraces her steps until she's disappeared.

"You've forgotten something," the manager mocks, turning the page back to Samantha with a twist of his braceleted wrist.

Oh. It's her signature. But as Samantha leans over, placing one scuffed shoe over the other, as the woman in the pen undresses again, she realizes she can't write it. Bizarre arthritis has struck and she can't move her fingers, not even to form one more word. She looks up at the man's implacable stare.

"I can't," she says, humiliated. Never to have exotic hair. Never to have crotchless underwear. Never to walk, perfectly, toward the door.

That night Samantha retrieves her stamp collection from underneath her desk. She scatters the little pictures on the table. She will put these in order. She will categorize them. She will date them. She will slip them in envelopes and seal them. She will do this if it kills her.

Samantha is thinking about sex. It seems far away, lost in a high school phantasmagoria:

You went into the bathroom and applied piña colada-flavored lip balm and took off your underpants and put them in your purse. You returned to his bedroom. You sat on the bed. You looked up at the Jimi Hendrix poster. You saw his hand move closer to your leg. You wept inside at the poignancy of it all. You took off your clothes like an Amazon warrioress. You asked: "What about birth control?" He said: "Don't worry, honey." You didn't. You felt like Carole King. You remembered the *Cosmopolitan* article that said sex could be used in any diet and exercise program, and you could lose the equivalent of 650 calories in ten minutes. You smoked a cigarette afterward, feeling thin and earthly. The man had your number and he was a high school senior. He didn't know where your underwear were.

These were the best of times for Samantha.

The buzzer to Samantha's apartment rings and she jumps, knocking the flora/fauna stamp section into world leaders.

It's Maggie. She's running up the stairs, out of breath. She's wearing a huge tan sweater—her father's? When she rushes past Samantha at the door she says, "Lock it?"

"Of course."

Maggie goes to the window as if looking for a CIA agent in a black car.

"Trying to shake someone?" Samantha wryly asks.

"My father is dead," Maggie says.

"Oh!"

"He was murdered."

"Oh, Maggie, but how? How could it be? He was just alive on Sunday, an old man, so friendly—"

"They murdered him because he had everything. They were jealous. Yes, they no longer wanted him to be free."

She's holding her sweater around her chest.

"Who are 'they'?"

163

"His nurse did it. She smoked all his cigars, too. She drank the whiskey."

"What was left of it from when we—"

"Don't talk to me! Something has to be done! Immediately!"

"What? What can I do? Anything, Maggie."

"We need to leave."

"Leave?"

"Go on a trip."

"Do you mean—?"

"I have a car, can you meet me in front of this building in one hour?"

"You mean, we can take a journey and look into the face of evil and come to some conclusion? You mean, we can travel and understand the wicked ways of the world?"

"Sure, Samantha, are you coming?"

"What about work? Tomorrow's Thursday."

"My father's dead! Murdered!"

"OK, Maggie, OK."

Samantha has packed her bag. She's got peppermints in there, panty hose, a book of limericks for the road. She waits at the street corner for Maggie. It's almost midnight. She kicks the snow off the curb. Maggie drives up in a Volkswagen Bug that looks like it's been around. She has a determined look, and Samantha realizes she doesn't even know Maggie's age. She used to think she was just a little older than herself, like a big sister, but tonight she looks forty.

"Can we call your friend in New Haven?" Maggie asks as Samantha clambers into the car, putting her plaid suitcase in the back seat, disrupting Stripe in the process. He growls faintly.

"Mark? Why?"

"We could stay there tonight, it's a couple of hours from here. Then we could get up early tomorrow."

"He's not really a friend, Maggie. He left me in a bar. He called me a child while we were in a stuck elevator. Besides, he only goes to school in New Haven. He lives in Brattleby with his mother."

Samantha says this while trying to find her seat belt. Maggie lurches into second gear.

The car isn't exactly, well, sturdy. Samantha stares ahead as they pass through the areas of New York City where, in nightmares, your car breaks down completely.

"Would you like some cheese and crackers?" Samantha says after a while.

"I don't eat."

So, Samantha decides *not* to get out her little snack pack, but she will brush her hair. She unhitches her seat belt and leans into the back. Stripe is sitting on her suitcase. She gently pushes him toward the edge. He yelps and bites her.

"Ow! My hand!" Samantha cries. "Bad dog!"

"Don't you talk to my dog like that," Maggie hisses.

"But Maggie, he bit me!"

"I don't care. Poor baby," Maggie says, reaching back to pat the evil mongrel.

Samantha casts Maggie a sidelong glance. Stripe has diffidently settled back down on Samantha's suitcase; Samantha's hair goes unbrushed.

"Help me out of my jacket? I'm hot," Maggie says a few minutes later. She extends one arm toward Samantha.

Samantha pulls at the leather stuff, finds it difficult to budge. She places a hand on Maggie's shoulder and pushes there as she tugs the jacket. Maggie feels disarmingly soft under all that black.

After a while, Maggie begins to speak:

"There is no choice. When the needle pierces your skin, when he enters without knocking the red-hot journey of your life. You'll do anything. He doesn't need to be told. He is gaining on you. His

165

fist rips into your belly and pulls out the life you've grown so attached to. The tear is slow and absolute.

"You wake to your cold bed in the dead white morning, and the dresser and the mail and the curtains are all less than horseshit to you. Your family tries to get you to eat, they bring you orange juice and tea. But nothing will do. That night, you stand at the window in your blown white nightgown. You wait. When will he return? That's all you need to know. Nothing matters but his teeth."

The headlights from other cars pass through theirs like beating wings. Samantha tightens her innocent hand around the door handle. She looks over at Maggie. Maggie's eyes gleam in the night.

The all-night restaurant is next to a family-style hotel, but Maggie doesn't want to stay there for some reason Samantha can't make out. They passed through New Haven with nary a word about Mark.

Sitting in an orange booth under fluorescent light, Maggie blows on her tea; the dark surface ripples like a lake. Samantha swirls the ice in her 7-Up.

"Where are we going?" she asks.

"Just going."

"Do you have a destination in mind?"

Maggie looks at Samantha as if she were a leaf.

"What is your friend Mark like?"

"Oh, well, he's perfectly suburban. He'll make a good husband, I'm sure. He's not at all what I want for my life."

"And what do you want, Samantha?"

"You know, something beautiful, blistering, hot."

Maggie snorts. She gets up and starts heading out to the car.

"Did you know if you drive too long at night your eyes fall out?" Samantha calls to Maggie's back.

✿

Early the next morning, Samantha wakes up in the passenger seat. The car is parked amidst a truck herd. Maggie is nowhere in sight.

Samantha's body feels like a skeleton that's been left in the back of a second-grade science-class storage closet. She's got her nightgown on over her clothes. Now she remembers Maggie giving it to her in the night. How sweet. Maternal even. The trucks hum ominously and it is freezing in the car. Samantha takes off her nightgown and throws it in the back.

She gets out of the car and proceeds to look for the cowgirl. But Maggie's not at the truck stop restaurant. Samantha sits down at the counter anyway and orders orange juice. She attempts a jaunty disposition. Ah, to travel across America in the middle of the night. To be in a town and not to know the name of it. To drop responsibility like so much tiresome silliness. After all, why should *she* be responsible? Leave that to the police officers and grade school teachers. Responsibility is just a concept made up by parents to maintain distance between themselves and their light green offshoots.

Fortified by such thoughts, Samantha leaves the restaurant and wanders over to the car. But what is happening there? Some commotion. Some steam on the window. Samantha opens the door.

"My nightgown!" she cries. Maggie is in the back seat and a truck driver is on top of her. Samantha can't stop looking at his big white hindquarters. They look funny, squeezed above his jeans like that.

"What the f—?" he inquires.

"Get out," says Maggie.

"But, Maggie—"

"Take Stripe for a walk."

Stripe is panting in the front seat. He looks at Samantha doubtfully.

Maggie's pulling the truck driver closer to her by the neck.

"C'mon, Stripe," Samantha says, turning away. Stripe hops out.

What would her grandmother have said? Samantha thinks, sitting on a picnic bench in the grassy triangle by the parking lot. She'd surely have pulled over to the nearest Christian intervention and free coffee center. God, a truck driver. A back seat! Someone she doesn't know, no first date. Did Maggie look happy, lying there, looking over his shoulder, staring at the car roof?

Stripe whines at Samantha's feet.

In a while, Samantha goes back to the VW. Maggie is sitting in the front. She's folded Samantha's nightgown into a neat square. Samantha and Stripe get in the car. Samantha puts on her seat belt. She sniffs at the air suspiciously. Maggie starts the car and they drive off.

"Don't you think we should have some ground rules?" Samantha says as the early morning sun becomes bright.

"Ground rules?"

"You know, don't smoke while the other person is eating, that sort of thing."

"This isn't a board game, Samantha. There are no rules to life."

And then Maggie retreats into a huge silence.

Samantha wonders what Bob would call this.

They stop often along the way (to where? Samantha hasn't the foggiest). The first stop is for doughnuts. Samantha calls her office. She doesn't talk to her boss, she talks to Mie-Mie, the secretary who answers the phone while Samantha is at lunch. "I'm very sick," Samantha says, holding her nose, praying that the ambient noise in the coffee shop isn't audible. Mie-Mie sounds disbelieving but cheerful, as if in collusion with Samantha. "No, really," Samantha protests.

Sitting in the car later, powdered sugar on their laps, Samantha says to Maggie: "I could live this way forever."

"What way?"

"Driving across the country, eating doughnuts, listening to cowboy songs on the radio. I don't want to be a secretary."

"You probably will be, anyway," Maggie says.

"Why?"

"It's written all over your face: 'I'll get the coffee. I'll type that for you. I'll come in early and organize your life into folders.'"

Samantha tries to swallow.

"That's not very nice."

"What's niceness got to do with it?"

She's probably upset about the murder of her father.

They turn in early at a motel. Samantha thinks this is a concession to her for spending the previous night in the car. She's willing to forgive and forget. On the other hand, Maggie could just be tired from staying up all night.

Snow flecks hit the window of their room. Samantha and Maggie are stretched out on matching beds; the crunch of the plastic mattress covers makes their silence apparent.

Maggie begins tossing more consistently.

"It's not right," she says.

"What?"

"It's not right to kill your father," she says, distressed.

"Did you say 'kill your father'?"

"I knew his colostomy needed attention. I knew his air bags were empty. I went into the kitchen and made a cup of tea. I went to the refrigerator and got a lemon and cut it in four. I squeezed the lemon into the cup. I stirred. When I came back, his eyes were marbles. I shouldn't have waited. I waited anyway."

"So there was no murderer?"

169

"I'm the murderer."

"But, you didn't kill him. He just died."

"You think you need a gun or a hatchet to kill your father? Try a long cup of tea for starters."

"What did the police say?"

"What police? I left him rotting there."

Samantha stares up at the ceiling. Flecks of phosphorescence in the paint are shaped into a heart: a cheap designer brainstorm.

"One shouldn't leave one's father dead and unburied in the middle of the city," Samantha manages. She tightens the floral bedcovers up around her neck. The whole world seems unconscionable.

In the morning, Samantha wakes up alone. That Maggie—she's an early riser.

Samantha looks at the thin, shockingly ugly curtains. These are the kind Mark Braun's wife will have in her kitchen. She will stare past them as she does the dishes. Her wedding dress will be in the attic, patiently molding. Mark Braun himself will sit in the living room, a sea captain encircled by his crew-member sons and daughters.

It's Friday, Samantha remembers. They must return to the city immediately and bury Mr. Cross. She'll then go to work on Monday. And Tuesday. And Wednesday. What then? What kind of life is this?

Samantha gets up and puts on her shirt and pants. She walks over to the bar/breakfast area off the lobby. Maggie's there. She's not alone. She's with a man. Who is this man? How can she find so many men in remote areas? Samantha can't find one in the entirety of New York City.

Samantha sits down. The man's name is also Sam—what a coincidence. He is drinking coffee; Maggie is smoking. She looked at Samantha—warmly? no, not warmly—when Samantha sat down.

"Who's this?" Sam, the man, asks. He's got keys jangling from his belt and little holes in his jeans from carrying change. He's got a scar on his forehead. From falling in love?

"She's my little sister," Maggie says. "She's a nun on vacation."

"Maggie, I have to talk to you."

"Later. Want some breakfast? Have anything you want. Pancakes? Bacon? Sausage? Grapefruit?"

Samantha orders eggs and tries to eat them. Maggie stares into space. The man, not wholesomely friendly, but apparently wanting something, swings his legs to and fro underneath the table. On the fro, one of his knees keeps hitting Samantha's thigh. She finds her eggs cold and unappealing.

"Ready?" Maggie says after a while.

The man gets up and gallantly puts down a twenty.

"Ready for what?" asks Samantha.

No answer. Maggie and the man, with Samantha trailing after them, exit the breakfast area and walk down the concrete walkway in the opposite direction from room 3, Samantha and Maggie's.

"Maggie," Samantha nearly whines, stepping around the laundry lady and her shopping cart, getting snow on her socks, "we've got to talk."

"You want to talk? Come with us. Otherwise, leave me alone."

The man unlocks the door to room 14; thank God he has a use for one of his keys, anyway.

Samantha thinks: I'm an adult. She follows them into the room. The TV is on, without sound. Clothing is strewn around. The Gideons' Bible is out by the channel changer. It smells like stale cigarettes and stale beer and stale room freshener.

"Is she up for a good time?" he asks Maggie. His hands are on her breasts. He snuggles up to her from behind.

"Sure, Samantha's up for anything," answers Maggie.

You know those movies where women cross themselves when they see something vile or cruel, death for instance? They always

171

have a sort of furtive, fake fear. Samantha finds herself mimicking the worst of these actresses when Maggie drops her tight black pants and the man enters her right there in front of her, right there on the floor.

Samantha backs up into the bed and falls over. The man and Maggie look like they are playing a strange game of Twister.

"Stop!" she whispers. Maggie's looking straight up at nothing, her face moving up, down, up, down. They don't hear Samantha.

She creeps closer and pushes the man's shoulder.

"What are you doing, babe?" he says. "C'mere."

"Stop it," says Samantha, a little louder. She pushes him again.

The man looks down at Maggie as if he has never seen her before.

"What's this girl doing? Does she want to be first?"

Not a rocket scientist, this Sam.

"Go on, Samantha, get out."

Samantha backs away. She picks up one of the man's work boots and hurls it at him. It grazes his ear.

He lets out a series of slurs and swear words. Maggie gets up and pulls on her pants. She comes at Samantha and pushes her out the door.

"What did you do that for, you idiot? How do you think we're going to pay for our room?"

"I have credit!"

"Yeah, and you'll pay for it with your little receptionist job. And you don't think *you're* a whore?"

Maggie rushes past Samantha toward their room.

Sam is at his door doing his belt.

"Cocktease!" he yells.

The laundry lady looks over. Samantha ignores Sam and tries to get in room 3, but Maggie's locked the door.

When Sam and the lady in white have disappeared, when Samantha's toes are numb from being outdoors, she leans up to the door and screams:

"WE'VE GOT TO GO BACK TO NEW YORK AND BURY YOUR FATHER!"

At this, Maggie lets the door swing open. She is all packed. She folds her arms and says to Samantha:

"Did you take my eyeliner?"

"No!"

"Are you ready to get out of here?"

"Where to, Maggie?"

"You're so set on going back to New York? We can go there."

Maggie never lets Samantha drive even though Samantha has a good record as a driver, even though she uses her seat belt and obeys all laws. Samantha has taken to smoking Maggie's cigarettes. She attempts smoke rings. She composes tirades to her therapist. "Bob," she begins, "did you know that I am a whore? Why didn't you ever tell me that? And what about drugs? Couldn't we try drugs? I mean, something is wrong here. My life is a shallow pool, a wading area for children and small dogs. Can't we get some goldfish? How about a plastic plant or a sea monster?"

When Samantha calls her office midmorning, Mie-Mie is charming as ever.

The Volkswagen has begun sputtering to a halt at the oddest moments: while passing cars, while at stoplights, while turning corners. Nonetheless, Maggie drives full throttle and sometimes even smiles at Samantha, who smugly imagines she's the cause of a transformation of sorts in this woman.

"Have you ever thought of doing any creative writing?" Samantha asks Maggie as they careen through Massachusetts. "It's a good outlet, you know."

"Give it a rest," says Maggie.

In New Haven, the car coughs, stalls and comes to a harmonious and absolute halt. It is eight o'clock.

They stand outside the car. They look at the highway. They look at the shopping mall. They wait.

A small car, domestic make, screeches to a stop two hundred yards in front of them. It backs up in a reckless crisscross.

Mark Braun steps out.

"Can I be of any help?"

"What an uncanny knack for coincidence, Mark."

"Oh, so *this* is Mark."

Maggie's smile is sweet.

"Mark, this is Maggie Cross. Our car has broken. Can you drive us to the train station?"

"We'd like to take you out to dinner first," says Maggie. Her voice is deep and resonant.

"We would?"

Maggie and Mark are walking on ahead while Samantha kicks stones on the way to the pizzeria. "Best pizza in Connecticut," Mark boasted, fluffing his ski jacket like a rooster's feathers. This is his town now, what with his one class at Yale. In Mark's car, Maggie lolled her legs around the back seat like vacuum cleaner hoses; she talked throatily to Mark in the mirror. Samantha stared ahead at the road. Now it has begun to rain. Cold hailstones ping off Samantha's nose. What could Mark and Maggie have to talk about so animatedly, intimately? Why are they leaning toward each other with such intensity?

It soon becomes clear from the way Mark cuts up his pizza into bite-size squares that he wants nothing more than to impress Maggie. He may have stopped the car initially as a samaritan's gesture toward Samantha, ex-sweetheart, but it wasn't long until he spied a new seduction—make way for *número seis* in his long and impressive roll call. Well, let him tiptoe forward like a captive ten-year-old walking the pirate's plank into deep waters, Samantha broods. He left her in a bar unattended. He listened to her heart-pour and remained unmoved (except to get off his stool, to leave the bar). He called her a child. Now this former Boy Scout is practicing a restrained flirtation with a woman who is too beautiful for even his wildest nightmare. Maggie. Who wouldn't want her? Walking around like a zombie from another universe, murdering fathers and what have you. They deserve each other. Amusing how life steps in and makes little mincemeat pies out of all your plans and desires.

Maggie says: "Mark, is there a place we can stay tonight? I'm too tired to go any further."

There is a darkness in her stare, her long arms lounging on the back of the booth go on forever.

"We could all stay at this motel I know, the rooms are cheap and good."

"That sounds nice," Maggie drawls.

Samantha tries to figure out the theme, plot and character development here:

1) A coincidence: Mark Braun, out of nowhere. She hates him, yet she feels he needs her protection against this black bear.

2) A betrayal: Maggie Cross, dream or reality, fact or fiction? Murderer? Friend of Samantha's? Nothing makes sense with her anymore.

3) A future: Samantha Brown, girl? Employee? Suburbanite? City slicker? Catholic? College graduate? Good citizen? Wife and mother? Sex queen? Hooker?

"Maggie," Samantha says in as measured a tone as she can muster, "we need to go tonight. We need to bury your father."

"He's not dead, Samantha. I was just joking."

"Joking?"

"What are you gals talking about?" Mark interjects nervously. The small pizza squares on his plate cool in the ensuing silence.

"I'm sorry, Samantha. Pass the pepper," Maggie finally says, shrugging her shoulders under the leather jacket.

Samantha walks outdoors.

✳

Little Stripe is tied to a fire hydrant. He is wearing one of his indomitable sweaters, a blue one tonight. Samantha stands in front of the restaurant and gazes out at the parking lot across the way. The dog, a few feet to her left, yips. Samantha looks over at him as if she were the Grinch Who Stole Christmas having an evil idea. She stalks over. She unties the dog. She says:

"Go on, you dumb mutt. You stupid, stupid hound. You knitted-together jumble of yarn."

She's pointing to the road, flailing her arms. Stripe wags his tail.

"You want to live, you wretched creature?"

He smiles—did she imagine that?

Samantha sighs. She sits down next to Stripe on the curb. He puts his head in her lap.

Maggie comes out of the pizzeria and sits down next to them— why, it's just like a family reunion. She launches into a new tale:

"My mother was a prostitute, not a German. She didn't go off with any one sailor, she went off with a hundred of them. My father wanted to marry her. When he found out she was pregnant, he paid her to have the child, and when I was three years old, she left me at his apartment for the last time and she never returned. He tried to find her on the West Side, where she used to work, but she wasn't there anymore. None of the other whores would talk to him about her."

There's something in Maggie's emotionless delivery that Samantha is knocked over by, and again she believes, or at least half-believes, or at least it doesn't matter if she believes, Maggie's story.

"Sometimes I wish I didn't have a charming, perfect savior of a father. I wish that I had a mother, perhaps, or even a sister. C'mere, Stripe," Maggie says, petting him.

"Maggie, I just tried to murder your dog."

"Don't be silly."

Mark comes out and looks down at the two women.

"I made the reservation," he says.

On the motel walkway, Mark whispers, "Samantha, I may have been too abrupt with you in the elevator. I'm sorry for anything I said that may have upset you. I still consider you one of my closest childhood friends. You'll be my friend forever."

He grins at her, earnestly, pleadingly.

Samantha returns his chickadee smile.

What do three people do in a motel room together? Mark, for one, sits in a chair, his jacket on, as if he's about to bolt out the door. Maggie files her nails. Stripe pouts under the table. Samantha reads all the literature on New Haven's cultural wonders. There is a mountain, a museum, a rock. It's quite a city, New Haven.

"Samantha? Would you do me a favor?" Maggie asks.

"Anything, Maggie."

"Could you get me Stripe's water bowl? I left it in the car."

Well, whatever happened when Samantha was gone remained unknown to her. Leave it to say that when she returned, Maggie and Mark were rearranged like pawns on a chessboard. Mark, no longer in his jacket, was lounging on the trundle bed; Maggie was in the shower. The unasked question of who would sleep where seemed to have been resolved. Samantha's suitcase was placed on one bed, Maggie's on the other.

Samantha goes to bed and pulls the pillow over her head. She hears noises, voices, and she steadfastly ignores it all. But in a dream, what goes on in the room is loud and clear. Mark and Maggie are playing pickup sticks on the floor.

"Maggie, you remind me of a flower, a peony. The way you are. It makes me feel that my life has meaning."

"Thank you, Mark," Maggie counters, sliding one stick out

from under another. "Just being with you gives me the jitters."

"I want to be a big man for you. I'll have a high-paying job and a secure future. We'll buy a country house with a gas grill and an electric bug zapper."

"I am and always will be an enigma. When you reach for me, sometimes your hand will go right through. I'll smile, but, like the Cheshire Cat, some evenings my smile will be all that's left for you."

"I'll have minor revelations and share them at dinner! I need a woman to come home to!"

"I am a woman. I need to sit by you. The life that doesn't include you is quiet, fragile."

"I'll inch over toward you!"

"I'll be at the bar, waiting. Silent, and forceful."

The sky is everywhere. What were once the walls of the motel room expand into horizons, directions—north, south, east, west. Every way Samantha looks the room is expanding into meadows and forests and oceans. The sky is so big and black, it's bright with blackness.

When she opens her eyes in the morning and tosses the pillow to the wall, Samantha discovers that Mark and Maggie are not at the motel anymore. Nor is Maggie's suitcase, nor is Stripe, nor is Mark's car.

Inquiring at reception, she discovers, too, that the room is unpaid for. She pulls out her credit card. She orders a taxi and takes it to the train station.

Samantha sits in a rear-facing seat on the train. Leaving the station, she is propelled back in space in an odd fashion. Her personal set of personality traits seem particularly hellish this morning. This would be a time for despair. Samantha staves it off by making a list. The first thing on the list is: find out if Maggie's father is murdered. If so, get him buried. Always good to bury a dead father.

178

⚹

Two important communications greet Samantha upon arrival.

On her message machine:

"Samantha? This is Mark. Do you know where Maggie is? We had to leave the motel early, we didn't want to wake you. We went to breakfast, and then we went to get the car towed, and there was a ticket on it. Maggie got nervous. I guess it isn't really her car. We had to—" Beep. The message is cut off.

And in her mailbox:

Dearest Samantha,

Nice picture, what a pretty smile. I have a big surprise for you, yes mam. I made parole! I'll be out on the weekend of the 16th. I'll come visit you and we can get to know each other better.

Love, Greg

After taking a shower, Samantha paces around the apartment preparing an outfit to wear. When she looks in her closet, the tag-sale array of fabrics and encumbrances looks less than interesting. She'd rather have nothing to wear. She'd rather have a red suede miniskirt. She had imagined donning such an item to visit Greg in Attica. However, he is getting out of jail—this weekend, in fact. This strikes her as unappealing, tiresome, trite. Aren't murderers, etc., better left off where they are? Part of the thrill of Greg—Scorpio with passion and style—was his encased aspect. Loose, he is without value. But . . . visiting her? This couldn't be the case at all, Samantha blithely assumes, laying out on her bed a tan pair of pants, a tan shirt, her ever-present white sweater.

She walks the streets she walked with Maggie. She finds the building where the potentially dead, potentially murdered father lives, or hovers. It is a sickly warm afternoon for winter. At the front entrance to the building, Samantha stares at the paint on the door. She runs her finger along the dozen or so names written by the buzzers. Johnson, Hatch, Bonski, Gabriel, Levitt, Smirnoff, Cross. Cross, Cross, Cross. 3B. It is one of the old engraved nameplates, the recent ones are cheaper. She buzzes. Almost instantaneously, Mr. Cross's voice booms out of the speaker:

"What is it?"

Samantha swallows. He lives!

"It's me, Mr. Cross, Samantha Brown, a friend of Maggie's. I was wondering . . ."

"Come in. But you'll need to get the key from Mrs. Smirnoff on the first floor, my dear."

It almost sounds as if he were expecting her.

Samantha gets the key from the superintendent's wife and trudges up the weird stairs. She, as Maggie had done, drops the key while fidgeting at the door.

She walks down the long hall. She looks into the bedroom. The man is sitting, more upright than last time. His hands are folded. His scary eyes disconcert Samantha.

"So, you've come back on your own."

"Yes. I'd like to ask you some questions about Maggie, if that's OK."

"Any question from an eloquent fawn will be answered with alacrity."

Samantha sort of smiles. Her veil of politeness, that which holds her together, seems transparent. She sits down in the little seat next to the old man's bed. The folds of his skin are like armor.

"Have you seen her recently?"

"Yes, she was here this morning."

"She was? What did she say?"

"Nothing unusual. Would you like a scotch?"

"Not today, thanks. Can you give me her phone number? I need to talk to her."

180

"No."

"No?"

"Her phone is out of order."

"What about an address?"

"I'm afraid I can't be of any help there."

"Look, Maggie is not in a good way, Mr. Cross. I don't think she's exactly happy."

"And you, you plan on making her happy, bunny Samantha?"

"I'd just like to be her friend." Not to mention ask her why she abandoned me with a motel bill and no car.

"Maggie can't have any friends."

"Why not?"

"She has no heart."

"Everyone has a heart, Mr. Cross."

"Sweet girl, a heart is a hollow basket to fill with chocolates. Maggie's heart diminished to dollhouse size when her mother and I divorced."

Samantha feels the breath leave her like when you are on an elevator that drops too fast, after being stuck on the tenth floor.

"Divorced?"

And in the next fifteen minutes, Mr. Cross tells Samantha a story of Maggie's childhood supplemented by photographs and documents. Ordinary would be one way to describe it. No vampires. No boat from overseas. No prostitute/mother. Maggie's mother, a secretary at P.S. 29, divorced Mr. Cross when Maggie was a teenager. Mr. Cross made his living selling encyclopedias. Maggie was an only child. "She loved stories," he says. "She liked to pretend she was an Avenger." After Mrs. Cross left her husband, she went on a ten-day casino cruise to Bermuda. There she met a man from Florida whom she later married. Maggie, as far as Mr. Cross knows, doesn't correspond with her at all.

"I don't know when she changed her name, either. It used to be Marian. She's really got a taste for the absurd."

✻

Samantha walks back to her apartment hunched over, as if she's carrying a baby bird in her arms. She needs to make a decision, something is hanging over her head. This strikes her as a new sensation. It isn't a mass of clouds, a whole future, it's a gnawing little thundershower. But what is it? What to do? Even slouching, she feels taller.

At first Samantha takes the man loitering in the hall to be an electrician or meter-reader. He's got the requisite blue outfit. He's got a pad. And he surely doesn't look like a friend of hers.

"Excuse me," she simpers and proceeds to unlock her door.

"Do you know Samantha?" he asks.

"Samantha?"

"Yeah—a tall, black-haired babe with long legs and a cute smile."

"Uh," Samantha takes a better look at this man. He's not tall himself, he's not thin or fat either, he's got brownish, nondescript hair, his eyes are small and, though not cross-eyed, not exactly focused forward, either. His shirt—Samantha swallows when she sees this—says: *My buddy went to Attica and all I got was this lousy T-shirt.*

Samantha takes the key back out of the lock and leans against the door.

"What did you say your name was?"

"Didn't say, mam. But my name is Greg. Are you Samantha's roommate?"

Scorpio? Rock and roll? Passion? Love? Oh brother. Perhaps Samantha isn't quite as interested in the heretical after all.

"Look, Greg. *I'm* Samantha."

"Ha-ha! No, the Samantha I want looks like this," he pulls out the picture Samantha stole from Mr. Cross's bedside table.

"Can I have that?" she asks, grabbing for it.

"No way! Who are you, anyway? Samantha's bodyguard?"

"OK, I'm the person who wrote you. I sent you that picture. It's not of me, it's—it's an old picture of a movie star."

"You're bullshitting me."

"No, I *was* bullshitting you."

"Well, I'll be goddamned. This is a bitch, huh? Here I'm out of jail for the first time in two years. I need to party, I want to show this beautiful woman a good time. Well, shit, I thought we'd go to Bill's. Say, you wanna take her place? You're not bad, though you sure don't look like that picture."

"No thanks. Next time."

Greg—murderer, love god, pathetic individual—descends the stairs, shaking his head. Samantha remembers something and leans over the railing.

"Say, Greg?"

"What?"

"What were you in for, anyway?"

"Mail fraud."

Oh, mail fraud. Nothing new about that.

It isn't until Samantha is in her apartment that her heart starts pounding and she realizes she was this close to a real live criminal, and that criminal was mad, and he could have murdered her— but then again, his weapon wouldn't have been an ax or rifle, but putting her in an envelope and licking her.

On the machine, Mark has called a second time. He pleads with Samantha to call him as soon as possible.

Samantha lies down and twirls her cross. Her bed feels like a new circle in the *Inferno*.

On Monday, Samantha steadfastly irons her prettiest floral dress—it's the dress she wears when she's feeling guilty, her submission dress. She puts on her panty hose. These have a run above the knee, but who'll notice? She puts on her black pumps, the ones with the heels that skid backward from overuse and gray, orblike discolorations by the toes. She only missed two days of work; good God, everyone needs a sick day. She's in before nine, positioned behind the pink crescent. She smiles at all incomers. She answers the phone on the first ring every time.

"Welcome back," her boss says upon entering. "May I see you in my office, please?"

The boss has her sleek pink blazer on, she's got a lot of jewelry. She's opening the lid to a paper cup and licking cream cheese from her fingers as she motions for Samantha to sit down in the visitor's chair.

"Samantha, we're going to let you go. I hope this isn't a shock. I just don't believe this is the right job for you. Besides, Mie-Mie found a stack of strange poems—does 'Samantha: The Life Story' sound familiar?—underneath the typewriter. I didn't particularly like being referred to as 'she of the tweezed eyebrows and hairy persona.' "

Samantha wishes she hadn't worn her submission dress today. She needs something bold—red, black or striped—to hold her own in such circumstances.

"I always liked your shoes," she wanly notes. "Do you think I should try another department?"

"Maybe another field?" the boss says helpfully, taking a sip of her cappuccino.

On her way home that evening, Samantha passes the shoe store. The help wanted sign is gone. She sees the shimmery image of the catlike woman behind the glass.

When she gets to her apartment, she takes off her dress and throws it on the floor. She opens the closet and stares at her clothing. She pulls out shirts, skirts, pants, and tosses them in a heap along with the well-mannered dress. She even throws in her white sweater. She off-shelves a ceramic cat, a basket full of dried flowers, a jewelry box with a ballerina stopped midway in endless

184

pirouette. From her bookshelf she extracts *How to Make Love to a Man, Sex Tips for Girls* and *Traveling on a Shoestring* and heaves them, too, on the pile.

Everything fits into two big plastic bags. She carries them out to the sidewalk. She stomps back up the stairs and, without thinking about what she is doing, rips the bedding from her saintly bed, and wrestles the lumpy old mattress downstairs, huffing on the way. She leans it against the garbage cans.

Wiping her brow, Samantha looks across the street. She sees a familiar black leg, a familiar black boot. She hears the clank of metal objects. Next to Maggie, beside himself with pleasure, is the mail fraud. Neither of them look Samantha's way, nor does she wave to the couple of the week.

Samantha squirms under her therapist's gaze.

"So, you had a little adventure?"

"Hmm."

"Who is this Maggie, anyway?"

"I don't know."

He falls into his "I'm waiting" silence.

"Bob, my sex life is nonexistent. I lost my job. I don't have a boyfriend. My family is distant as the moon. I'm tired of living as if there is good and bad and nothing in between. Everything is in between, it seems to me now. My grandmother was wrong. I also hate panty hose."

"Interesting."

"What's so interesting about it?"

"Your face is flushed today."

Samantha meets Maggie in Tompkins Square Park. She had called, whispering hoarsely that she needed to talk. When Samantha arrives, Maggie is sitting on a bench, rocking back and forth, smoking a cigarette. She glances at Samantha from behind her lock of black hair.

185

The empty benches and long, wrought-iron fences look lonely on this cold afternoon. A middle-aged woman watches her dog play in a dirt patch. A teenager sits by the entrance of the park, looking out. Two ancient men in black suits play cards and talk in a language Samantha doesn't know. It sounds as if they are commiserating about injustice. Maggie sighs, stamps out her cigarette and says: "I went to church the night before last. God is a voyage with no end. You can do penance to him. He is cruel, very cruel. I like that. He is consistent. Better than any man I've had."

"Is cruel good?"

"Cruel is very good. But—"

Samantha waits. Maggie stops rocking for a minute; she looks down at Stripe, sitting at her feet.

"I think your friend Mark likes me."

"Well, you seduced him, no doubt. That would have been around when you left me in the motel, alone, to pay the bill, with no car."

"I couldn't help it."

"Oh? Just like you couldn't help lying to me about your father, about your whole life."

"I *want* to want a man like Mark, good husband material. I like what you said you don't like about him—you know, that he's boring, conventional. I want to try to have a normal life."

"What about Greg? Isn't he more your type?"

"Yeah, I'm at Bill's and all of a sudden this ex-con shows up. Good going, Samantha."

"So you want to be a suburban housewife?"

"I had a dream last night after I went out for ice cream with Mark. He found me somehow—they always do. I dreamed that I was in a house with no lights. The snow was crusty on the porch. There were no footprints, long like the triangular, pointy-toed boots vampires wear. No bat shadows in the rafters, no blood drops on the mat by the door. I put my hand to my throat: still fresh, smooth, unpunctured. Then I remembered: Dracula isn't

186

coming home anymore."

"You don't have to lie to me, Maggie."

"There's nothing left."

"Don't you have a self?"

"Do you?"

Samantha reaches for her crucifix. A self? She threw it out with her ballerina jewelry box. She reaches further up, to her hat, the one Maggie gave her. She touches the fur to reassure herself.

"If I went away, would you take care of Stripe for me?" Maggie asks.

"Are you going away?"

"I give him a raw egg with his meal at night. If he starts scratching, put some cottage cheese in, too. He only wears sweaters when it's freezing or colder out."

Maggie gets up.

"And he gets a multivitamin once a week."

"Maggie, where are you going? Come back!"

She is walking away, Stripe following in her wake. But when Maggie's gotten close to the edge of the park, as Samantha calls out again into the winter air, into the cool city, Maggie disappears. Completely. Like a piece of Saran Wrap, a two-dimensional figure, a photograph—as if she never existed in the first place.

All that's left is a scraggly little dog ferreting around the trash.

"She's disappeared," Samantha patiently explains once more to Mark, as they sit knee to knee in the same bar he left her at one memorable night.

"No one just disappears," Mark says, also patiently.

Samantha is feeding olives to the grayish canine at the foot of her bar stool. The dog barks greedily between mouthfuls.

"She wasn't your type."

"You're just jealous."

"She wouldn't have been right."

"She was perfect."

"I don't know what happened to her. You weren't good for her."

"Damn, I was good for her! She made me feel like a million bucks! She knew what to do for a man! Unlike you, Miss Lay-It-All-On-The-Line Weirdness."

Samantha makes shapes with a stringy thing before her, the crucifix on its thin chain. She picks it up and folds it into itself again like a snake.

"Maggie didn't have a good relationship with her dad. She was too nice. So she had to be mean to everyone else, including herself," Samantha says, trying to make up a story to convince Mark.

"Look, I know you're in therapy, you told me that on our first date. But that doesn't mean everything comes down to psychology. You know? I mean, Maggie was—is—a beautiful woman. She needs a man like me to protect her. I don't care about her stupid father."

"Mark, listen to me. Maggie is gone. Get it? The only thing left is her dog. Now, if you don't mind, I'm going to the bathroom. I'll be right back, all right? Relax. You've got a beautiful nose, remember that. C'mon, Stripe."

Samantha puts on her leather jacket and saunters out. She's forgotten—forgotten?—the crucifix.